The Gig Harbor Suicides

a novel by Ashdon Byszewski

March 2016

for erin and rachael,
my big sister and my angel

Man is not what he thinks he is, he is what he hides.
– André Malraux

before

Parker

"Parker. Parker." Someone was shaking my shoulders.

"Hey. Park. Parker."

Sirens. Sirens. Too loud. Too much light.
I felt a warm hand on my side, but I didn't have to turn around to know who it was. Josh. By the rigid tone in his voice, he was trying to be the brave one. But everything was fine. Why was he doing that? Nothing was wrong. I looked around. Why was I lying on the filthy street, curled up in a ball? What was wrong with me?
I sat up dizzily, brushing my jeans off. Down the street a little ways away, I saw two ambulances, a firetruck, and a police car. Mason was talking to a paramedic, a sick look on his face. Lux was standing off to the side, crying so hard that she was hiccuping. Loudly. Mascara was running down her face in runny black clumps. I'm sure if she knew, she would've stopped. But why was she crying?
"Josh?" I heard myself say. I frowned after I said it. My voice sounded high pitched and timid. Was that what I sounded like?
He immediately was at my side. "Yeah?"
"What.. happened here?"
My voice was so slow now. I kept looking around, looking for anything that was wrong. A clue. A hint. Something.
Josh inhaled deeply. I didn't like the look on his face. "You don't remember, Park? You passed out. Do you remember anything?"
His voice was tinged with something I couldn't quite recognize. He was holding back on something, obviously. I ignored him. I saw my hint. Four paramedics, walking past the entrance of the Rockefeller center, pushing a

stretcher to the ambulance. There was a body on it, but I couldn't tell whose it was. It was covered with a white sheet.

My heart jumped. Somebody had died here. Holy *shit*.

I continued to watch them for a couple more minutes, breathing too fast, until they loaded the stretcher and body into the ambulance. As they fumbled with it for a second, the sheet shifted up, and I saw a pair of black converse poke out right before they closed the doors. Black high-tops.

My stomach lurched for a second. I felt like throwing up. My breath caught in my throat. Never in my life had I felt so sick.

I glanced around, the world pounding through my head.

Mason. Lux. Josh. Me.

Mason, Lux, Josh....

"Josh?" I choked out. High pitched. I didn't care. I didn't care. My head was hurting so bad. So bad.

This time, Josh leaned down and sat next to me. He looked at me, really looked at me in the eyes, a tug of war between brown and blue.

"Where's Charlie?"

Josh looked down for a split second, then back up at me. His eyes got very, very dark. They went from his usual dark brown and straight to black. It wasn't a scary look, but for some reason, my heart dropped to my feet. I was out of breath in a second, because his look told me exactly what I was most afraid of.

But that was ridiculous. Charlie was fine. He was probably still inside. What the heck. He was fine. Everything was fine.

"Josh. *Where is Charlie.*"

He wouldn't look at me.

"No. No. Nonononono."

I stood up, pushing Josh's arms off of me, my legs shaking below me. The ambulances were starting to pull away now.

I could feel myself slipping into full-blown hysteria before I fully realized I was already hysteric.

Charlie? My Charlie? No. He was okay. He was fine. It wasn't him.
Everybody has those shoes. It didn't mean anything.
But my body moved anyways.
"Charlie?" I called, shaking. "No, wait! Wait! WAIT! CHARLIE!"
I blindly ran after the ambulance, screaming as loud as I could, but they
were quickly picking up speed.
"Charlie! Charlie!"
I screamed his name until my voice was hoarse, sprinting. Inhale, scream.
Inhale, scream. Charlie Charlie Charlie.
I don't remember when I fell, but it's probably a good thing I did. Running
out into full on New York City traffic wouldn't have been pretty. Did I trip
over something? Did I collapse? I wasn't weak. I'm not weak.
I felt hands again, this time under my arms. Josh was picking me up.
Holding me up. Telling me to please stop crying, yet he was crying himself.
I was crying? He called my name a couple times. I think I heard him say I'm
sorry.
Why was I letting him hold me back? I wanted Charlie. I needed Charlie.
Right now.
Charlie was.. dead? Charlie? My Charlie?
My best friend was dead?
No. No, that was impossible, because I'd just had breakfast with him this
morning. That was impossible, because Charlie was my best friend Charlie
was here and alive and fine, Charlie was okay, and okay seriously Parker
come on there was no way that was Charlie under that sheet.

Charlie.
I don't remember what I thought after that. I just wanted to hear him talk,
saying anything, knowing he was fine.
The street felt better against my side. I wanted to lie down again.
Let go of me, Josh. I want Charlie.

after

Parker

I'd never been to a funeral before.
She didn't want me to come. My mom. Actually, she flat out told I wasn't to go.
But I needed to. I had to come, I told her, because I just had to. I didn't owe him, he didn't need closure or anything like that. It was just that he was Charlie, and I needed to come.
My parents didn't want to come, even though Mrs. Collins' invited my whole family. Never cared for funerals, my mom said. My dad was still asleep. So, at exactly eleven thirty in the morning, I stepped out of my little blue truck, and onto the walkway of Harbor Life Church alone, heading into the place where I would see Charlie for the last time.
Before I walked through the doors, I allowed myself to look around the grounds for a minute, soaking in the smells of the harbor.
I thought about Josh, kneeling next to me on the street.
I thought about Lux, crying for twelve straight hours.
I thought about Mason, numb to it all.
And I thought about Charlie. Charlie, my best friend, the happiest, most radiant person I knew, who had jumped to his death, leaving us behind forever.
Charlie, who had killed himself.

Walking inside, I left the cool air behind me and entered the enormous lobby. They were holding the funeral outside, since the weather was nice. Personally, I just thought it was because the inside was too happy for such an event.

There was a slew of people everywhere I looked, some searching for the Collins, some holding flowers, and some just talking amongst themselves quietly. I overheard an older couple with two little kids remark how it was convenient that the New York Times kept his death out of the papers, being as it was so 'tragic' and all.

I noticed that everyone was wearing black. I guess that's traditional. I fingered my own black dress self-consciously, glancing around just as nervously.

Why was I nervous, though? I had every right to be here.

But at the same time, I didn't, because Charlie didn't deserve to be dead.

"Park."

Josh sort of half-smiled at me when I caught his eye. He was wearing a dark grey button-up. I was secretly kind of shocked. I'd never seen him in anything but sweaters and flannels.

"Hey. How are you doing?" I asked quietly, my voice audible only to him. Behind him, by the entrance, I saw Mrs. Ethan and Josh's little brother Kyle walk in, looking around slowly.

He shrugged one shoulder, up then down. "I'm fine. Have you seen Lux and Mason?"

I sighed. If Lux were here, we would've known by now. "No. Want to go outside?" I wasn't in the mood for small talk. Or any talk, really. I just wanted to get this over with.

Josh glanced at me out of the corner of his eyes. His expression seemed to soften somewhat, then he said of course, and so we headed to the church garden for the ceremony.

Lux

White lillies. Those were his favorite flowers. It only seemed.. I don't know, right, to get some for today.

My parents decided to go early to save a seat, so it was my job to chauffeur myself and my little sister Juliette to the funeral.

I stopped at the florist to grab a bunch, then drove over to Harbor Life Church, almost late. I thought about the white dress that I'd chosen to wear today, instead of black, in representation of Charlie's white lilies. It would stand out, like Charlie had.

That was the entire point.

When I parked, I stared at the bunch of lilies for a couple seconds before unbuckling my seatbelt. It was what Mason would call melodramatic, but for some reason, I couldn't get the lightning white image of lilies out of my mind.

Juliette was silent the entire ride there. She seemed to grasp what situation we were in here, what was going on around her. I was glad. Normally, she was a bit of a nuisance. But today, she was grown up and urbane. I was proud of her.

I reached over and lightly touched her arm, smiling gently. "Thank you for being so good today. It means a lot to me and The Collinses. Mom and Dad are proud of you already."

She looked up at me, her face a blank, white little canvas. Her little button nose wrinkled, her teardrop-tiny mouth furrowed. She adjusted her black headband amidst her dark locks and then looked up at me.

"Does it hurt?" She asked quietly, seriously. Juliette was not one for dramatics.

My immediate reaction was to say no, of course not, I'm fine.

I drew in a short breath, taking my arm back, holding the vase tightly.

Yes, it did. It *hurt* missing Charlie. It hurt knowing he was gone.

"Yes," I finally said as I opened the door to the car. I'd been delaying going in. "And I think it always will."

Everyone was already sitting down. I scanned the crowd for Mason and Josh and Parker. They were sitting in the front row, right next to Charlie's parents. My own parents were a row behind them. Juliette slid in next to my mom. Parker was right next to Mrs. Collins, face stony and her eyes nonmoving and unfocused. Her body was rigid, sitting straight up. She was sitting on her hands. Josh's eyebrows were knit together, and he looked around the entire setup thoroughly confused, the way you look for something you're not sure how you lost. He rubbed his eyes and blinked slowly, then looked around again, seeming to remind himself that this was even real.

Mason was sitting low in his chair, his legs spread apart in his typical stance. He looked over the crowd, and when he saw me, he ran his fingers through his hair and smiled with half his mouth. It would be typical, but his gaze didn't stay on me, heavy and clear, like it usually did. His dark blue eyes darted around, to me, then to the coffin, then to the ground, and back to me.

"Hi," I said, quietly. Mason was, as expected, the only one to answer.

"Where were you?" he asked, almost sounding a little ticked off. "You were almost late."

I held up the vase of lilies. "They were his favorite."

He just sighed.

Parker

"Charlie Tobias Collins. Our brother is finally at peace with the Lord." The pastor announced solemnly.

It was time to say our goodbyes. I, along with Lux, several of Charlie's family members, and people from around the area had decided to speak. Mrs. Collins said we didn't have to, that He knew what we couldn't say, but still, it felt right to say something. He was my best friend, after all.
I strode stoically up to the front of the casket, staring down at the dirt and rainbow of flowers and other mementos we had thrown in.
A picture of the five of us, on our first day of senior year. My arm is slung around Josh's waist, Charlie's shoulder, and Mason is holding Lux like a baby.
A picture of Charlie and Lux on a boat at Lake Washington.
His favorite book.
A ragged, pasty green, falling-apart blanket.
The lacrosse stick his parents had gotten him when he made Varsity.
A gold necklace he'd gotten me for my birthday one year.
I hadn't been able to look inside the open casket.

Charlie. Charlie. So many memories, school, home, my dad, my house,

"Parker, Parker, it's okay, come on. Let's go."
I am frozen on my doorstep, hearing my father screaming from inside the house and my mother yelling back just as loud. We both flinch as the sound of something heavy hitting the wall echoes around to us. Most likely, a frying pan. That's what my mom usually grabbed when my dad was in one of his stupors and she was getting scared.

Charlie yanks on my elbow gently. "Park. Just stay over at my house. You can call them later. My parents would love it. We can just relax, watch movies or something."
When I still fail to move, he tries again, this time succeeding.
"Come on. You don't need to be around this."
He leads me back to the car after another minute of convincing, and after I'm buckled up, he reaches over and hugs me tight.
"I just want you to be happy, even for just a little while. Parker-"

"-Parker? Would you like to speak?"
The pastor smiled kindly at me.

I shook my head the tiniest bit, clearing my thoughts. I nodded, semi-sure of myself.
I stepped up to the front of his casket, looking straight up at the hazy blue. Everyone else had looked down when speaking, as if they were talking to him.
I couldn't bring myself to do that.

"Charlie... was..." I tried, my throat cutting off my words.
And I knew I couldn't do this, and in that moment I hated myself.

"Charlie Collins was an angel." I finished calmly.

He *was* an angel. My angel.
My angel.

My last word echoed around in my head, repeating itself in its finality.
My angel….. gel….gel gel gel….

The word echoed, ricocheted, banged up and down across the enclosure that was my head. I knew that. I knew what that meant. No. Not today, not now.

I smiled forcefully, then walked back to my chair. I felt blood rise to my cheeks, wondered how many people knew the real reason I had to step down. Maybe Josh. Lux. Mason. Charlie's parents, maybe. Maybe.
One would think I would be used to this by now, used to public humiliation and the prickling you feel in the small of your back, almost exactly like the feeling when you can feel everyone staring at you. But in fact, it's the exact opposite. Nobody's looking at you, intentionally. They're looking everywhere *but* at you. They're scared to look at you. They're scared of you.
Scared of *me*.
"Don't look at her," an unfamiliar woman's voice said from somewhere behind me.

I knew what my psychologist would say, that I shouldn't hate myself for something that I couldn't control, that I shouldn't let other people's judgments get to me. "They don't know you. They don't even know your illness. They don't understand that it's not your fault. *You* know that, the people that know you best know that, and that's all that matters." I could just hear it.
I closed my eyes and sank into my chair in embarrassment. Mason looked at me sideways, a quizzical expression on his face.
But that woman. She sounded like she was talking to a child, protecting them. From me.
Wait.
I spun around in my chair, looking for a woman I didn't know with a kid. I knew everyone here.
"Yes, *her*," the voice said again. It still came from behind me.
Then it hit me, again. No. Not now, please, not now, seriously. I felt tears, hot in the corner of my eyes, begging to run down my face. My heart was pounding. My throat hurt from the lump that was steadily growing in it. I blinked it all back. Not now. Please, no. No. I'm here for Charlie.
Not now.

And his name echoed around the room, floated through the air, all around me. CharlieCharlieCharlieCharlieCharlie, in counts and beats I couldn't make out, whispery dark voices blended together that I couldn't analyze.

"Stop." I whispered under my breath, feeling the panic rise to my throat like bile. I thought about the coping skills.

Screw the coping skills. It was too much. Everything was too much it was too bright outside the wind was too cold it was too *much.*

The whispering didn't stop.

"Stop it. Right now. Stop." I said again, this time more forcefully.

It got louder, faster, and I closed my eyes and tried to tune it out, pretending it was just white noise. I fought the urge to squeeze my eyes shut and scream.

Josh

Parker was breathing heavily, her eyes closed most of the time, looking around her frantically, terrified when they were open. It looked like she was on the tipping point of a panic attack or something. Her head didn't move at all, so people behind her didn't notice how nervous she was.

Then it dawned on me. Parker was having one of her episodes, right now. She wasn't crying, but her icy blue eyes were darker and even harder than normal.

She was trying to stay stony. Trying not to seem upset. But the act was only believable from her neck down.

I stayed calm. I reached over Lux, ducking my head.

"Hey, Park." I touched her arm gently. The black fabric was warm, despite the cold sun.

"Do you want to get out of here?"

Parker

Josh noticed something was wrong. I was horribly embarrassed. Why was I so unstable, so scared? After a couple minutes of terrified, rigid ignoring, the voices went away and the echoing succumbed, and I hadn't heard anything else, but the possibility was there, haunting me. I was so scared and ashamed and mad at myself for being so weak.

I breathed in, then out, gathering my emotions just enough to appear normal, like I was upset because of my best friend being buried and nothing else.

Josh looked at me. Not at my pale face or that I was sitting on my hands to keep them from shaking, but at me. Into my eyes.

If Charlie had been there, he wouldn't have asked me if I was okay, because we would both have known that I would say yes but mean no. He'd been around during several of my slip ups- always making sure I was okay.

He wouldn't have asked me anything, because he would know that I really didn't like to decide how to answer when I was like this.

He would say "Let's go," quietly, to me only. Not in a condescending way, like he was just helping me to prove to himself how nice he was. Not annoyed. In a way that let me know that he had noticed that something was wrong, but somehow just made me thankful that he cared enough to notice. More thankful than upset that I was open enough to *let* him know.

He would have done exactly what Josh did.

Josh

Looking at Parker like this hurt.

I led her away from the church, her face pale and drawn. She never really showed much emotion whatsoever, but still. She was messed. The fuck. Up.

We sat haphazardly under a gigantic pine tree in front of the church, our backs to the water. I pulled a crumpled pack of cigarettes from my pocket, lit one, and inhaled greatly. Jesus, what a train wreck.

I'd never really even see her have an episode. I knew what she had, and honestly, I didn't really care. It wasn't her fault.

It wasn't even the fact that that had just happened. It was the fact that I'd never seen her so upset, so raw. I mean, granted, one of our best friends had never died before, but I'd never seen her this much of a mess. She was a mess right now, and it hurt to look at her. It really did. It felt like my insides were all twisted up.

Looking at Parker like this hurt.

She was sitting at my feet, crouched into a tiny ball. Her breaths were rapid and shallow, and honestly, I was a little concerned. Should I call someone or something?

Then she turned around, her face pale, even her freckles, her nose red, her pallid eyes dark and swimming and heartbroken.

"Why'd he do it, Josh? Why'd he do it?" She choked out, completely and entirely sad. There really was no other word for how she felt than sad.

I broke all over again. I could literally, actually feel my heart shattering into tiny shards of glass, penetrating my insides. Parker. Oh god, Parker.

She looked for all the world like a little girl. A little girl who was vulnerable to everything.

I leaned down, sitting in front of her, trying desperately to think of something, anything I could say that would protect this little girl.
"I don't know, Park. No one does but him. I don't know why he did it, especially where we were. I don't know, Park. I really don't. And I know you're not okay. But I'm right here, okay? Whatever you need, I'm right here."

I could at least be here for her. I could do that much.

She was quiet for about an hour. People started walking out of the church, heading back to the Collins' house for the repast. She watched them all leave with vacant eyes.

I lit another cigarette. Who knows how long we'd be here.
"Can I have one?" Her timid voice rose up.
"What- oh, yeah, of course," I stumbled, caught off guard for a second. I handed her my own.
She took it gracefully, and I saw her lean back against the tree instead of bundling herself up in a ball. In that moment, I wanted to grab her and tell her she would be okay, she *would*. God, I just wanted to protect her and keep her safe from the whole world. I wanted her to *know* it would be okay. It would. Charlie was gone, but she was still here, and she would be okay. And I was here. I would make sure she was okay.
I glanced over at her, the only side visible to me; her back, clad in her black scooped dress and near-white hair. As the smoke drifted up, past her chin, past her ears, past the tree, I wondered what she was thinking about.
I just hoped she was okay.

Parker

I remembered us flying home from New York. It was a quiet journey- no one spoke much. Maybe we didn't have much to say. Maybe we had too much to say but didn't know how to get it out right. Maybe we just didn't want to say anything.

Mason dropped us off at our houses back in Washington, first Lux, then Josh, then me.

I remembered how sick I felt the closer we got to my house.

I remembered I waved goodbye to him.

Then I walked in my house. My mom was sitting at the counter, cooking dinner in our dingy, crowded little kitchen for her and my dad.

I remember looking at the cutting board she was slicing carrots on. And the pot of water on the stove that wasn't boiling yet. And her. She looked at me, dropped the knife, and staggered over herself to hug me. There was flour on her jeans.

I remembered this feeling washed over me in that moment, a feeling that I couldn't quite place, but I would later look back and realize it was despondency in the raw.

I remember I let her hug me for a full ten seconds, then I couldn't, I just couldn't handle her arms around me any longer. If I allowed her arms to be around me for one more second I would quite literally throw up the entire contents of my stomach all over her.

I speed-walked to my room down the hall, closed the door, and dropped my bag. Then I reached down and picked up said bag, and unzipped the little tiny pocket in the bottom where Josh and I used to hide cigarettes when we were younger. In that exact pocket, I pulled out a tiny purple bottle and shook out exactly two orange sleeping pills.

Sleep. I remember that I just needed to sleep this off. Sleep was what I needed. Right now.

I remembered taking said pills dry, swallowing hard. Then I remember laying down on my tiny bed, holding the bottle to my nose. I remembered that it still smelled like cigarette smoke, and it was a nice smell, it calmed me down. My ceiling was very nice, I realized more and more as I stared at it. It was painted dark blue and had those glow-in-the-dark stars that little kids stick up there. Some were pink. Some were orange. Blue. Green. Yellow. Purple.

Then I remembered nothing, except his name, Charlie's name, over and over and over, coming from a place outside of me, echoing, playing and replaying itself in the room like a tape that's been rewound again and again.

Parker

The thing about my psychiatrist appointments were that they were always so inconvenient. Smack in the middle of my morning or afternoon or evening. Always right in the center of something, almost as if it was trying to get at me, like, *yes! This is your psychiatry appointment that you require because you're mentally disturbed! This is the most important part of your day! You can't ignore it!*

But, nevertheless, I *could not miss them.* It had been drilled in my brain for many years, and even now, the fact that they were so damn necessary still ticked me off.

So, as I drove to Delphi Psychiatry that morning, I couldn't have been more indignant. I didn't want anyone with me. I just wanted to go in and get out as quickly as possible.

As it were, my appointments were never short.

I was so used to the grey building that by now, I could probably find my way there blindfolded. It was only about twenty minutes away from my house. Cliche, sure. But the truth, yes.

I parked in front, reluctantly shutting off my music and exiting the comfort of my car. The sky was getting semi-darker now, and a nice gust had kicked up.

The weather here was almost therapeutic for me. No matter how much I had adored New York, Washington would always remain with me.

As would Charlie. Anyways.

Attempting to push all thoughts of him out of my mind, I walked into the blue and beige waiting room. The lady at the front desk smiled at me. I didn't even have to go up to sign in anymore. I was a regular here at Delphi.

I sat down in one of the polished leather-back chairs, criss crossing my legs. A little boy was playing with the box of legos on the floor, the same exact box, in fact, that I had played with many many years ago.

"Parker?"

I looked around the corner. Dr. Schress had his head poking out from behind the door. He was smiling.

I got up, abandoning my thoughts, and the faintly chemical smell of waiting rooms. Time for the inevitable.

The nice thing about Schress and I was that we never kidded around. He was cool. And we didn't just talk about my medication. We only had one hour, once a month, yet he always found time to ask me normal questions, about school and friends, not just about my issues. I expected my mother had already filled him in about New York, but nevertheless. That was good. I didn't want to think about it, much less discuss it.

His office was large and airy, and had one of the best views I'd ever seen- a huge, rectangular window that took up nearly the entire wall, overlooking the harbor.

I took my usual seat on the wooden stool in front of the window, and I felt myself relax slightly. Tension seemed to fall off my shoulders and neck as I heard the AC kick on, and cool air filled the room.

Dr. Schress leaned back in his trademark brown leather chair, smiling up at me, his pen positioned precariously on his lip.

"So. You've had quite the month, haven't you?"

I fought the urge to laugh, but the sarcasm evaded me anyways. "You could say that. My best friend's offed himself on our vacation, and I couldn't speak at his funeral because I had an episode. So, yeah, lovely April so far."

Schress didn't always take notes during our sessions. Usually, we just talked stuff out. But today, he had his computer on, and was already typing away with his back to me. I knew better than to try and read what he was putting up by now.

"It sounds to me like you're feeling guilty because of what happened at the funeral." He commented lightly.

"Well, yeah. It was my fault. I could barely talk. It was ridiculous." I admitted, swinging my legs roughly against the wooden rails.

He stopped typing, and instead reached for a pad of paper and a ballpoint pen. He didn't look at me yet.
He tapped his chin with the tip of the pen. "What happened at the funeral, exactly? Did you hear the voices again? Have you been seeing things again?"

I told him what had happened. Just the whispery voices, and the woman. The only thing, I told him, that I was grateful for, was that I hadn't actually *seen* anything. Normally, the voices weren't violent. But the hallucinations always were. When I was little, I used to hallucinate all sorts of terrifying things. Thank *god* I didn't anymore.
I used to think that I wouldn't see or hear *anything* when I was older.

"Get it away from me!"
I'm screaming at the top of my lungs, voice garbled by tears and terror, huddled in the corner of the living room, my hands over my eyes. I am six years old, and terrified out of my freaking mind of the creature by the couch.

My mom is uselessly standing in the room, sobbing loudly, holding her arms across her chest.
"Parker, there's nothing there! *What is wrong with you? There's nothing there, honey!"*

I am still screaming, crying, completely having lost it. Do they not understand that it's *right there behind them? Do they not see it?*
My dad is absolutely furious, or maybe just concerned.

23

"Parker. Look at me. Look at me. There's nothing fucking there! Snap out of it!" He snaps his fingers at me, which just makes me cry harder.
He looks at my mom, red faced and completely at a loss for what to do now. She just looks at me, clad in my little pink t-shirt with the hearts on it and green shorts, barefoot, having thrown my shoes at the creature in hopes it would go away, and she tries to motion to the couch, trying to show me that there's really nothing there. It just makes me scream more, don't touch it, don't touch it.
"I think we might have to just take her to the hospital, Tim." My mom says, dropping her hands in defeat.
I am screaming louder, louder now, my feet curled up to my chest as I struggle to inch away from the creature behind the couch. It's moaning at me, and it's still looking at me.
It's grey. It's ugly. It's hunched over, clawed. It's awful. It's a thing most kids would only see in nightmares. And it's looking at me, smiling.
I continue to wail and wail. Why can't they see it and why aren't they doing anything? It's looking at them, too.

I almost laughed at my own wishful thinking. It was so ridiculous. *Just kidding, Parker, you're going to be a nutcase forever.*

Schress paused for a moment, ignoring that dig at myself.
"Parker, you've been on the Risperidone for thirteen months now?"

I nodded once, sitting on my hands and swinging my feet lazily. "Yeah. Why?"
Last time he had asked me about my medication, it was because he'd lowered my dosage to see if it would help.

"It says in your report that you've been experiencing more symptoms as of late."
It wasn't a question. He swivelled his chair around to face me.

"So here's the deal. With your disease, any kind of traumatic or severe event can trigger the episodes, sometimes into what we call 'blank periods,' despite being on medication already. It's sort of like you're detaching from reality. When Charlie committed suicide, did you black out at all, or forget what happened?"

My tongue was stuck to my throat. Son of a bitch, my medical mysteries just seemed to pile up, didn't they?
I remembered Josh waking me up. Shaking me. Asking what happened.
I numbly nodded my head.

"So that was a huge trigger. Your mind couldn't handle it, so it shut itself off. I'm going to take a wild guess here and say that his funeral was also a triggering event, yes?"
I nodded again.

He sighed slowly, stroking his brown-stubbled chin and fixing his glasses. "I talked it over with another one of my colleagues here. You've been on antipsychotics for psychosis-based schizophrenia since you were eight, Parker. Eight. By now, you should've had it under control, or at least been experiencing very, very little side effects.
"But you aren't. If anything, they've gotten worse. We've tried lowering your dosage. We've tried upping your dosage. Risperdal has worked for many people, Parker, but it might not be the right fit for you."

I didn't say anything. He wasn't done.
"Here's the thing," Schress said, sighing again, "You've been a very.. individual case for Delphi. And the Risperdal showed signs of lessening your episodes... once. But now, it's acting up again." He glanced at his computer. "You had thought echo, disorganized speech, and motor behavior, all in the span of two weeks?"

"Yeah." I let out a single, heavy breath. I didn't tell him about the hallucinations. The woman at the funeral. Seeing and hearing things, period, wasn't going to help.

"*That* tells us that it isn't working. So, if you consent, I'm going to start you on Clozapine."

"What's the difference?"

He smiled at me again. A good sign.
"Clozaril, the more common name, is a bit more heavy duty, for more serious cases. Abilify was what we had you on as a child, because it isn't as strong. Risperdal more recently, because as you got older, you required a stronger medication. But now, you're eighteen, and your body and mind can handle it. The only side effects are dry mouth and shakiness."

I straightened up in my chair, picking up my head from the window. For some reason, I felt drained. So, so tired. When I spoke, my voice was duller than the color beige.
"That's fine. Sounds good."

Schress gave me a sort of sad smile. "You're having a flat affect again, Parker. Just because this disease is frowned upon doesn't mean *you* will be frowned upon. You aren't a problem."
"In fact," he smiled at me. "You're a pretty good kid in my book."
Jesus, Schress. I wish.
I *did* wish, incidentally. All the time. On dandelions, on 11:11, on birthday candles, on everything. I knew it was childish, but then again, I'd always been a sucker for wishes.
I wished I didn't have schizophrenia, constantly. Whatever birth defect that had caused me, I wish it had been abolished. No one in my family had it. I was just a fucking defect.
I wished my parents would figure their shit out. I wished people at school

weren't so ridiculous. I wished my dad didn't drink and get so angry. I wished my mom didn't succumb to him. I wished Dr. Schress could get me on a medication that actually worked for once. I wished Charlie hadn't killed himself.

He handed me two papers to sign, and although he was so sure this would help, I wasn't sure I was. I knew I'd have this forever. Thirteen years of being a freak.
Thirteen years of Parker the schizo.
The hum of the AC dulled. The scratching of my pen rolled away. Even the sounds of the harbor were lulled. Yelling, yelling…. Too loud of voices. It was just me and my mind now.

"Get the fuck out of here, schizo."
Boy number one corners me. His buddies are coming in from all sides now. They are the Nazis of seventh grade.
I will myself to be uncannily strong. Block it out, forget about them, they don't matter,

"Are you fucking listening? Or are you too retarded to understand us?"
A single shove, hard, to the floor. I'm caught off guard, not paying attention. My elbows slam into the tile, and the pain shoots up my arms and causes spots to dance in and out of my vision.
Just shake it off, Parker, shake it off.
"Get the hell away from me!" I yell back, kicking out. My foot connects, hard, into somebody's shin. A cry of pain, then a searing agony in my forehead.

"Don't take it personally, schizo. We just can't have a psychopath like you in our school. It's not safe."
And now they're hitting me wherever they can reach. I'm so, so tired, I'm not fighting back anymore. I should be. To everyone around, it looks like I'm the victim, the weak little girl who is too scared to stand up for herself.

But I'm not weak. I'm just tired of it. All of it. I'm letting them use me like a punching bag.
"You're going to kill me!" I scream. I can't help it.
Then I really am screaming, and it hurts so bad, please stop, please stop..
I faintly hear running, louder voices. Two teachers are here now, yanking the boys away, leading them away. I still hear them as they go.

"Ooh, she's upset, Tyler. She's mad now!" He laughs, rearing his leg back. "She's such a fucking freak. They shouldn't let her be around everyone else."
As they are led away, and the bystanders with them, I slump into a little ball against the lockers, shaking. It was bad enough that it got out, that everyone knew. But now, I was That Girl. The one that everyone looked at funny, or walked the other way when they see. Even the teachers glance the other way, sometimes. They didn't used to. If something happened in class, they dismissed it. Now, it was all everyone looked for.
I hurt so bad, all over. But I won't cry. No. Don't cry, Parker, don't cry. Don't you dare.
I steel myself, wiping my eyes furiously, the lump in my throat hurting so bad as I attempt to swallow it.
Another person walks up to me now. I'm focused on their shoes. Black Chuck Taylor's, high tops. Mud all over them.
I don't want to look at their face again. If it was one of those guys again, I'll just look away and take it.

But this person slows down when they get close. They bend down, and then sit down on the floor.
It's a guy, but not the same one that was harassing me. Never seen this one before. Messy brown hair, warm brown eyes. Longest eyelashes I've ever seen. Looks like he might be my age. Loose fitting jeans and a dark green flannel. He looks like the kind of person everyone would be comfortable with.
And he is looking me right in the eyes.

"Hi. I'm Charlie. Do you want to get out of here?"

Not, 'Are you okay?' Not, 'Should we go to the principal?'
Not even, 'You're that girl everyone thinks is crazy.'

Do you want to get out of here.

Parker

I would not cry in front of Charlie's parents.

On my way home from Dr. Schress's office, I got a call from Mrs. Collins.
She had a box of some of Charlie's things she thought I would like to have.
Oh, christ.
I said yes, of course, I'd be there as soon as I could. Charlie only lived
fifteen minutes away from me, tops. I'd had his address memorized forever.
I was so tense. I caught myself clutching the steering wheel too tight, so
hard that my knuckles were whiter than my face. I was humming to myself,
some song with lyrics I couldn't make out. I drove slowly down the pretty
much empty street, mentally calculating the house numbers; 3318, 3319..
3320, Rosedale St.
I started to breathe only through my nose, mouth clenched tight. I always
did it when I was upset.
Relax, Parker. It's a box of stuff. Chill out.
But it was *his* stuff.

I pulled into the Collins' driveway shortly after noon, and smelled someone
cooking barbecue as I got out of the truck. I hadn't realized how hungry I
was.
Charlie's family lived in a super nice, super sunny neighborhood called
Rosedale, with big houses and wealthy people, mainly old people. There
were always cook outs and birthdays and extravagant cocktail parties
around. I'd been to a couple of them. My favorite had been the day one
summer when we'd hosted an enormous neighborhood water balloon fight.
It was insanely hot that day, and we had nothing better to do. Charlie and I
had won, and his mom took us out to ice cream to celebrate our victory.
Granted, we played against mostly adults and toddlers, but still. We were
eleven.

I was trying to remember what flavor ice cream I had gotten when Mrs. Collins opened the front door, smiling too big to be real.

"Parker! Hi, sweetheart."

She was carrying a cardboard box, big enough to fit a small pony. Her hair was tied up in a straggly bun, but was coming loose with today's wind. Her blouse had a large, dark spill all down the front, and so did her shorts. She caught me looking. "Water," She apologized. "I was gardening out back."

I bit my lip, taking the box from her. Charlie's mom had a huge garden, filled with every sort of flower you can imagine; coneflowers, catmint, forget-me-nots, daisies. She spent hours out there while Charlie and I swam in Lake Crescent or rode bikes or devoured boxes upon boxes of popsicles. One time, when we were younger, we'd actually chased the ice cream truck for three miles. We were both suckers for ice cream.

Every time we were at his house, Charlie used to pick a forget-me-not every day and stick it behind my ear, despite his mom's instructions of never pick my flowers.

I wondered now how long her garden would last, or if she'd even bother tending to it after a couple weeks. Did it matter anymore?

We sat down on the sidewalk. She didn't seem to want me in the house. Fine by me. I wasn't sure I *could* go in there.

She opened the flaps gently, dirt underneath her fingernails. She smelled like fertilizer, like Home Depot or something, and sunshine. Kinda how he did. He always smelled like fresh fruit that had been left out in the sun for too long.

"It's just a couple things Jeff and I went through and thought you might want. Some mementos, knick knacks, that sort. Letters, too." She smiled softly, almost chuckling. When we were thirteen, we had pretended to be secret agents for a month, sending each other letters written in invisible ink or in code. After a week or two, though, we gave up. I couldn't believe he'd kept them.

But right after she'd started to laugh, her face crumpled like a paper bag, and it broke my heart to remember that not only had I lost my best friend in the world, but she'd lost her only son, too.

Without another thought, I plunged headfirst into the box of Charlie's things;

His polaroid and favorite film with the rainbow edges.

The secret agent letters.

Pictures of him and I from vacations in Seattle and Lux's family's beach cabin, and then just him at his grandparents in Montana.

Valentine's Day cards from looooong ago, the candy grams bearing things like "Have a sweet day! xoxo, Lux." Or "You've got my heart. Love from Park."

Four of his favorite records: Everclear, Nirvana, Billie Holliday and Vampire Weekend.

His lacrosse jersey.

A small, green, raggedy old bunny rabbit, the stuffing coming out in one foot. Tally.

Every single object I touched sparked a new memory, a raw, unopened one, and I felt my throat getting tighter and threatening the break.

No. I would *not*. Cry.

"Thank you, Mrs. Collins," I forced my throat to cooperate. "This means a lot. Thank you so much."

She patted me on the back gently, rubbing her hand in big circles, casting her eyes downward from the sun. That just made me squeeze my eyes closed. No one had ever done that to me, actually. Charlie preferred hugs or light touches.

"Of course, sweetheart. You're welcome here anytime, you know that? We love having you over, Parker. Anytime."

She was smiling for real now. Her eyes had a tiny tug in the corners, wrinkles that were fading into exhaustion.

I just nodded, not trusting myself to speak.
Their house would be so empty now, wouldn't it? The sun had gone out.

As I carried the box back to my truck, I could feel the oncoming wave of sad and I knew that if I didn't get out of there fast enough it would be very bad. So I tried to be as quick as I could, my movements jerky and rough. I fastened my seatbelt quickly, one hand on the wheel, one hand on the box, like I was protecting it.

Mrs. Collins waved me goodbye, turning around to walk back into her sunny, airy, empty house.
Then she doubled back. "You know, Parker, you're allowed to miss him in front of people." She said suddenly, shielding her eyes from the sun.

I had to grind my teeth to keep from sobbing. I nodded at her grimly, hoping she wouldn't be offended. The last thing I needed right now was another sob fest, another person holding me, telling me it would be okay.
Because nothing was okay. Charlie was the only person who made me really believe things would be okay.

She walked back into the house. The second the door was closed, I let my forehead drop onto the steering wheel and allowed myself to miss him, once more.

Mason

I could feel them all staring at me.

Cole, Tommy, Daniel, Jake, all of them. As someone pulled off a sweaty jersey, or stuck their helmet back in their locker, I could feel their eyes on my back, watching.

What were they looking for, anyways? A sign? Maybe a tear, slipping down my cheek, a little mark of hurt, a sign of weakness? Bullshit. They were gauging my reaction. They were trying to see if I was like him, if I had "issues" that were going to make me kill myself too.

Jesus christ.

I pulled my white t-shirt over my head, then turned around to face them. As soon as my eyes hit theirs, they looked away, at the ground, or into their duffel bags, as if they hadn't just been stalking me with their gazes.

I waited for someone to say something. Anything.

Nothing.

Just then, Coach Green walked into the locker room, his face pulled back into what we called "The Reaper." He was a middle-aged guy, but when he was sporting his resting face, he looked like he was on his way to deliver the world's worst news.

I wondered what the news were this time.

"Boys," He said, nodding to the ones brave enough to make eye contact with him. They all ducked their heads respectively.

"Gray. Come with me, please." He said.

I followed him.

Inside his office, he asked me to sit down and offered me a coke. I accepted gratefully.

"So," he said calmly as I sipped cold bubbles. "How're you holding up?"

I put on my best game face. What had happened to Charlie was a fluke, a totally random occurrence. It didn't mean I was like that.
 "I'm fine, coach."

Coach Green nodded. "That's good to hear. Sports really help us channel our emotions, don't they?"

I fought the urge to throw that back at him. Charlie had played lacrosse, and clearly that didn't help.

He continued. "I know it must've been tough, coming back to football and stuff after what happened to your friend. If you need to take a leave of absence, the team will understand. However long you need, Gray."

I felt the fight rear up in my head. Not anger at him, really. More like anger at Charlie for getting me into all of this crazy shit. Thanks, buddy. Way to take one for the team.
And it wasn't just me. Did he really think Parker would handle this well? Or Lux?
I knew that they said suicides were often well thought out plans, one that the person had thought of for a long time. But that was bs. Because clearly, Charlie hadn't thought about us. He hadn't given a damn about the people he was leaving behind.
It was selfish.
"Coach, I'm not quitting the team just because my friend died. No way."

Coach Green looked over me once, nodding to himself. Then he stood up, and I took that was my cue to leave, too.
He clapped me on the back heartily. "That's what I like to hear. You're a good kid, Mason."

I thanked him, and left his office as quickly as I could.

Thank god the rest of the team was already out of the locker room.
Jesus.

After I put my stuff away, I called Lux, checking to see if we were still hanging out tonight. Go get dinner or something. Our anniversary was in a couple days, and we'd had stuff planned out for every day leading up to it.

She picked up immediately. She was crying.
"I-I'm sorry, babe. I am. I'm so sorry." She tripped over her words, apologizing over and over and over.

I tried not to sigh. She cried and whined too much to me. "It's fine. But hey- are we hanging out tonight or what?"

Lux hiccupped. "I don't- I don't know, Mason. I think I just want a night by myself."

I clenched the phone tighter in my hand.
"Okay, whatever. See you soon."

She said goodbye and I hung up.

Jesus christ. Why was it that I was the only person in the group who could handle myself?

Parker

I drove for about 45 minutes to Twanoh State Park. It was one of my favorite places. My Grandpa Rudy had taken me here when I was little, and he had a baby blue paddleboat that we'd take out onto the lake and fish and swim off of.

We talked about little things the whole way, things that fooled us into thinking that we were just two people. Normal people. Friend group 100% alive.

Now, normally I hate small talk. I liked to be meaningful. But with Josh, it was different. Somehow, everything he said seemed relevant and interesting, and he had a way of listening that made me feel like everything I said was meaningful. I guess you could say that it felt like *talking,* not just filling up the empty space in the car with emptier words. Even if the most insightful thing we talked about was the sunset.

Which, by the way, was beautiful. The clouds were blushing a pastel pink that faded into yellow as they approached the horizon. Each cloud had a distinct silver lining, and behind it all, you could see the flow from yellow to blue to purple to black, if you looked East.

By the time we got there, it was completely dark and the clouds had blown away. I couldn't help but smiling.

"This way," I said, sliding out of the car and heading to the tiny footpath that stemmed from the parking lot.

Josh

She led me silently through the narrow and windy path. It was off-season, so there wasn't a human anywhere: no squealing kids playing tag, or slightly older kids getting drunk and howling as loud as the could into the night, or large groups of rednecks turning their redneck music a little louder with each beer, or any of the noises I associated with campsites.
Parker was quick and silent, not pausing at a fork in the path, not tripping over roots. I could easily tell she had been here many times before, and it was all I could do to keep up in the pitch black. Especially with my added burden of the blankets, but I didn't want to interrupt her while she made her way through the woods. She seemed so happy, so sure of herself, which was a side I never saw of Parker, but it was a beautiful side to be sure, and I'd do everything I could to keep it showing.
After an uphill and downhill trek, Parker stopped. We stood at the end of the line of trees, and I could see the lake that Twanoh was famous for reflecting the silence and darkness. For a split second, I wondered if we were lost, if we had taken a wrong turn somewhere and ended up at the wrong place, but she said, "We're here," her voice a breath.

She started off again, and I followed her straight up to the water, to a dock whose gate we slid around easily, to a faded blue paddleboat. Parker undid the lock while I climbed in.
We paddled out to the middle of the lake. It was quiet, but for crickets and owls and our own breathing, a little heavy from the paddle out. The water was dark and glassy. I could feel her warmth.

"This is nice," I said, looking at Parker. I was completely used to the dark and I could see her perfectly, her eyes smiling back at me.

"Wanna know the real reason I come here?"

We climbed over to the back of the boat, where we could sit more comfortably. She sent me a quick and grateful smile, and I followed her eyes up to the sky.

There were stars, more than I knew you could be seen from this planet. The longer I looked, the more I saw. Diamond dust sprinkled across the black velvet of the sky, a dazzling fireworks display paused just as the sparks began to dissolve, billions of pinpricks in the heavy blanket of the unknown.

She spoke up again. "I just really like the thought that no matter where you are, we're all looking up at the same star patterns in the same sky. Isn't that comforting? It's like you're never too far away from someone."

I felt something grow in my throat, a feeling that was warm and sunny and beautiful all at once. It wasn't that Parker had just shown me her secret place, it was that she knew I would've loved it.

We sat for a long time like that, looking at the stars, feeling each other's presence, warm and calm and right beside us, listening to the night: the high-pitched lull of the crickets, the occasional whoosh of the wind, the low and smooth call of an owl.

Parker leaned on me, like she always does, and when she spoke, her voice was the melody line of the chorus of the night, the center note for the chord of crickets and wind and silence.

"Thank you," she said. That was all. But it was everything. I knew what she meant.

"No," I breathed into her pallid hair. "Thank *you*."

And she looked at me, in a way I couldn't quite decipher. In a way that was quiet and loud all at once. For a fleeting second, I wondered if Charlie could see our stars wherever he was.

And I looked at the stars and smelled her cocoa-and-cinnamon smell (she smelled like all the best parts of Seattle.) and thought about how even though it seemed like she was my whole world, there was a whole lot of world out there that wasn't mine.

Josh

Titlow Beach had always been a sore spot for me. When everyone else went to dingy bars and dark houses after parties, I had always come here. It was a quiet place. I liked it. So it made sense that, given the circumstances, it was the place I wanted most.

I took my converse off by the shore, leaving them half buried in the sand. There was no one else here, probably due to the current weather: it was absolutely pouring. I loved it.

Crawling under the wooden beams and over the rocks, I nearly lost my footing in the icy water twice. God, I would hate to be in there right now. Even the boats in the distance looked uncomfortable.

The smoking hole was close by. We'd made it up as kids. If you crawled under the pier far enough, there came a point where the rocks sloped downwards, and there was a little hole that nearly lapped the water's edge. You couldn't see much once inside, but it made for a great little smoking spot. You had to be quiet though, because the old man that patrols the top of the boardwalk can spot teenagers anywhere.

I treaded the rocks carefully, trying to keep my one free hand above water, as it held my cigarettes and lighter. Finally, I saw it.

The smoking hole, alone, was a thing of innocent beauty. Green, black, brown, and blue just kinda jumped out at you. And it was so peaceful. A little cul-de-sac of peace, in a way.

Since there was no one here, I ditched the actual hole and just settled myself on two of the smaller rocks. Leaning back, the rain half missed me. My pants would get thoroughly soaked, but my face would remain dry for now.

I stretched my legs out, my jeans rolled up as to avoid the water, and lit up. As I went to pocket the little blue lighter, I stared at it a second too long before hastily putting it away. Huh.

Oh, yeah. Parker had gotten it for me for my birthday last year. Along with this hoodie. Grey, simple, with one black stripe across the chest. It was my go-to rainy day attire.

Parker. Hm. Parker. The smoke arose from my mouth, mixing in with the swirly grey sky.

Parker. I wasn't even sure anymore what that name meant to me. In the past two weeks, I'd seen more of her than our entire friendship. She openly broke in front of me. That was trust. If Parker wasn't trust, then nothing was.

She trusted me. She let me hold her. She talked to me.

Parker. What was I even saying?

What was Parker, anymore? She was still just Parker. But she was different now. I was different. I wasn't sure how. Nothing had changed. Used to be, we could hangout whenever. Hell, we just went to that campground yesterday. But something felt off. Right now, if she were here...

Suddenly I was aware of how warm I was despite the cold air. And how I'd been trailing off without meaning to.

Oh, shit. Shit.

The campground. The way she looked at me differently.

My legs felt more numb to the rain than before.

I thought about how when she had grabbed my wrist so I didn't topple over, and how it had felt like there was a searing heat throughout my entire body.

I knew exactly what had changed.

I liked Parker.

That was it.

"I'm sorry, you'd
was irritated.
I suppressed a sigh
"Yeah. Sorry about t.
abruptly.
Two years. I'd been wit
reservation in Seattle, at
Every single anniversary,
always her choice. Which v
But I was getting at myself. I
lately, with her, with us.
How could I break the news to .
Lux wouldn't do that. She would
contrary, she would probably pret
problem. She would just go all icy a
so her.
Canceling our anniversary dinner was
rather break the news over text or some s...
when she's all excited and dressed all nice…
Damnit Lux.
I put my phone down on the bed, leaning back into my pillow, rubbing my
hands over my face.
It shouldn't be this hard. Being with someone, I mean. She was gorgeous.
Those long, perfectly toned legs, perfectly straight brown hair, propelling
green eyes…. I mean, she was insanely hot. And she was great at
everything she did.
But she was so *clingy*. And with all this stuff with Charlie, she was even
worse.
Yeah, I wasn't about to do that.

, and opened iMessage.

ta break up.

ιs, with different approaches, before just realizing I
.ι was good. Yeah.
ιnging. Ringing.

ggravated. "Hey, I'm kinda busy right now. What's up?"

ιotta talk." No time to mess around here. For either of us.
ιper voice immediately downed. I could picture her face: crestfallen.

ιout?"

I didn't feel at all remorseful. "We're done. Sorry."

I couldn't hear anything but empty ringing. I considered hanging up.
Then, after a few awkward moments,
"What?"
Not crestfallen: shocked.

I opened my blinds, and not a single thought of Lux, Charlie, or any of them bothered me.

Parker

It happened in Tacoma.

According to the weather app on my phone, it was going to be sunny and warm, completely cloudless today. So, upon waking, I dressed for warmer skies, and took off before anyone else had even woken up. Incidentally, it was already nine, but my father was lazy and my mother had work.

It was foggy and grey outside, but I told myself the sun would be good for me. Brightening my spirits and whatnot. So, reluctantly, I resorted to my six-year-old habits and actually said goodbye to the trees and forests and harbor, and headed for Tacoma's Antique Row.

I loved it when I was younger. Charlie, Lux, Josh and I had spent hours at a time wandering through the many stores, buying pointless junk, occasionally sneaking away from the others to secretly buy them something. Charlie had once gotten me an Everclear record, which had turned out to be warped. We all pitched in and got Lux a little blue dresser she had her eye on, which she still had, right next to her bed. I got Josh an empty pink cigarette carton once during his rebellious days, in the shop I was convinced was haunted. It had a fairy on the front and smelled like strawberries and dust. He called it gay and proceeded to laugh about it good heartedly.

As I parked my truck haphazardly, that brought another through to my mind. One that I'd been steadily pushing away without noticing. It snuck up on me during quiet dinners in my dingy kitchen, in the awkward moments that ensued during therapy appointments where no one spoke, in the little snatches of thought right before I fell asleep.

This thought had faded blue jeans and white converse that I'd once tied their laces to my own during a concert in Seattle.

Josh.

I got out of the truck, and sure enough, the sky was a deep blue, reflecting off the buildings in a way that made me feel safe. They closed in on all sides, and there were people everywhere.

Josh.

Without meaning to, I saw what I wanted to. What could happen. Josh and I, over the many years, had been close. I'd knew him. I understood him perfectly. A lot of the time, it was like we were on the same rhythm. We'd even slept in the same bed together. Okay, it was my blue tent, camped out in the woods, but still. He'd carried me before. He'd taken care of me, like any friend should. He'd always been there. And recently, he'd been there in ways that really counted. As I'd been there for him.

The sun suddenly felt too hot on my face as I grew nervous. What kind of feelings did I have for him, exactly?

Enough to want to find out, the little voice in my head replied coyly.

Yeah, no.

Or yes?

Not yet defeated, I made my way to my favorite store, a five-story building, each level littered with small shops, crammed and overflowing. When I was thirteen, Josh and I had climbed out of the baby blue window on the fifth story, sitting on the shingles and watching people enjoy their days.

I wondered what would happen if something *did* happen. I'd never had a boyfriend in my life. Thanks to Charlie, my social status was stable, but I was still the crazy girl. No boy wanted to get with that. Probably afraid I'd freak out and go all redrum on them.

As it were.

I didn't even realize where I was until I was there. Fifth floor, blue building. I hastily avoided an employee and skirted past boxes and machine parts until I got to the window.

I brushed aside the cobwebs, and lifted the frame up gently. There was a cool breeze that pushed my hair into my face, just enough to make me shiver in the shade.

Enough to make me wish Josh was here. He would have put his arm around me or held me until I wasn't cold. He was never one for the whole here-take-my-jacket thing.

I felt myself blink. Wait.
And that was when I knew. It was Josh I was wishing were here, not Charlie.
That was when I realized that maybe, just maybe, things could be okay again.

What a thought.

Josh

"So. Is dinner at The Smith tonight okay with everyone?"

Charlie grins, standing in the doorway of our hotel room, lazily leaning against the frame. He's still dressed in his usual: a flannel that was way too big, jeans that were also way too big, and black converse hi-tops. It almost looked like he was trying to hide himself, to lose himself. And that probably would be the case, except Charlie was larger than life, and he knew it. And he liked it. The clothes were merely just another quirk about him.
On the other hand, I was the opposite. My style was very alike to Charlie's, except nobody ever compared the two. It was always Charlie's thing, so that made me the one who looked like I was hiding.
I look down at my shoes. Blue converse. Charlie's were black.
I smile to himself. Not everything has to be the same between us.

Lux pokes her head out of the bathroom, a fluffy white towel wrapped tightly around her willowy frame. Her hair is dripping all over the floor.
"Is that the super fancy restaurant we were checking out yesterday on 3rd?"

Charlie smiles at her. "Yep. If it's alright with you guys, I'll call and make the reservation right now."

Lux nods, delighted. Mason agrees too, saying he really just needs a cheeseburger. Parker, who's been sitting on the corner of her and Charlie's bed, says "Sounds wonderful" With a tiny smile on her face.

Charlie ducks out into the hallway, cell phone in hand. Less than five minutes later, he emerges again. "We have a reservation for five at ten o'clock."
Then, as an afterthought, "Dress nice, everyone."
Parker snorts.

"Park? We're leaving in ten minutes. Are you ready?"

She's laying on her back, hands crossed over her chest, eyes closed. She has earbuds in.

I pull one out gently, putting it in my own ear. It'd been our little thing since forever. If one of us was listening to music and didn't answer the other, then we had the right to listen with them. Plus, I knew full well not to bother Parker when she was daydreaming. But I didn't really mind, anyways. Her face gets this peaceful look on it when she's daydreaming. Like she was somewhere far, far away from here.
An happy sort of sunset-vibes song hums quietly in my head after I put the earbud in.
"She's got the rays of the sun now
Flowing through her hair as she turns around
And the waves of the sea rising up underneath…"
Parker's favorite band. I've heard the song before, and I think it might be her favorite one, but I can't tell for sure. Her music taste is incredibly vast and endless, going from stuff like Blackbear to Yellowcard.
She hums along, quietly, barely audible. "If you look into my eyes you'll see I'm alive…"
We sit in silence for a couple minutes, me sitting quietly, Parker seemingly asleep. When the song ends, she still doesn't move. Her chest rises and falls, slowly, slowly.

"See I'm Alive. The Mowgli's." She suddenly announces, seemingly to nobody. Her eyes are still lightly shut.

"Good song." I comment lightly. She doesn't seem to be that awake yet. Honestly, I'm not even sure if she's here, mentally.

Then her eyes snap open, and she sits up slowly.
"I never want to leave this moment." She announces, in a quiet little voice that she only took on when she had been really thinking.

I exhale. Sometimes, I just didn't understand her.
"How come?" I ask, vaguely intrigued and also slightly annoyed. She always gives these vague little answers, never just the straight-up truth.

She sighs, then grabs my hands and pulls me right in front of her. We sit with our legs criss-cross, knees almost touching. Almost.
Her hair is sticking up all over, and her freckles look almost lopsided.
And here Parker puts one hand on my knee, like she has something very important to tell me all of a sudden.
"Because, Josh. In this moment, I am completely and utterly happy. I am sitting here, in a nice hotel, with the view of my dreams, with my favorite music, and with you in front of me. I am alive. And I am here. In this moment, I am happy. I am in freaking New York. I am with my best friends. I'm far away from home. I'm happy. I'm just really really happy."

A smile escapes before I can help it. Would you look at that- a full answer, no vague notions here. It was so adorable. I loved hearing everything that went on in her head, even the messes in her mind. I loved it. When we were younger, maybe fourteen, she would just pull me aside out of the blue and tell me about her newest adventure she'd planned, or dream she'd had. At first, I always wondered why she chose me. Not Charlie, not Lux, me. But now, in this moment, I think I got it-
It was because I listened. And I cared.

"I'm glad, Park."

*She traces lazy circles along my knee, looking deep in thought yet again.
She glances out the window, looking out at her favorite view again. All
those lights, all those cars, all those buildings.*
*Then she looks back at me, sighing again. She drops her head forward,
right where her hand had been a second ago.*
*I don't know what to say. So I just play with her hair, like I always do when
she's sleepy or scared.*

*"I should probably put something else on for dinner, huh?" She asks, her
voice muffled by my knee.*

*I glance at her outfit. She's wearing a little white sundress, one of the
straps falling off her shoulder. I'd never seen her wear it before. Probably
because back home right now, it was about thirty degrees. A sundress
there would result in death by freezing.*
*She's all crumpled up by sleeping. No shoes. Her toes have purple nail
polish that's chipping off on some parts. Hair in straggly curls, falling
messily over her back.*

"I think maybe shoes. Otherwise, I think you look-"
*Then I stop myself. I had been about to say beautiful. But that sounded
almost too sweet. We weren't together, nor would we ever be. Just Josh
and Park till the end.*

*"Carefree. You look carefree. It suits you." I finish instead. It was true,
anyways. She looks like a girl that went wandering and wasn't sure where
she'd ended up.*
Parker lifts her head up slightly, smirking at me.
"Ha ha. I look like I just woke up. Don't lie to me."

"Well, you did just wake up, didn't you?"

"Shut up."

And with that, she bounds off of the bed in one leap, and into the enormous walk in closet the hotel room had come with. The second her head disappears out of view, I bury my face in my hands.

Sometimes, Parker was overwhelming. She was just wild. One second, she's asleep, the next, she's a freaking firework. All sparks and ideas and dreams. It was her mind. Her mind was a vast horizon of oceans and ideas and dreams.

It wasn't carefree. It was beautiful.

And as I pick at a loose thread on my blue flannel, I can't help but think that sometimes, I really just didn't get Parker, despite having known her for three years.

But then I remember that was the whole point.

Josh

I hadn't talked to her since the funeral. Something had to change, and right now.

The thought of actually seeing her, in person, feeling like this, made me a bundle of nerves. I couldn't even handle calling her. I just wanted to see her.

I sent her the most vague, indifferent text I could've done. We'd hungout at my house a million times before, and hers the same. Titlow beach. I could be calm there, hopefully not acting like a total freak. Yeah, I could be calm there. Hopefully she could be too.

She replied within ten minutes. *I'm in Tacoma rn. When do u want me to be there?*

5 pm? I responded. I was calmer at night. So was she.

Sounds great, see you then(:

I had never been more excited to see Parker. I felt like I had been injected full of liquid sunshine. I'd known her for four years. But the thought of tonight- just us, like we always were. Park and Josh. Just how we'd always been.

I knew every single thing about Parker. I knew how that her favorite color was blue, but the kind of blue that the ocean was. I knew that she was obsessed with ice cream but most of the time couldn't finish it. She hated purple jelly beans but loved every last green one. Her first day of fifth grade wasn't perfect, but the sunset that night was. She'd never seen fireworks in her life. When she brushed her teeth in the morning, she danced to She Way Out by The 1975. She liked music better than art. She wanted more than anything to travel the world. The one time we played Never Have I Ever at Lux's house and she said she'd never kissed anyone, Charlie had laughed and kissed her cheek and I had felt so left out that s*he* had

54

laughed and kissed the top of my head, which is how I knew she liked those better. She always slept on the left side of her bed so she could look out the window as she fell asleep. She loved loved loved the Museum of Glass. She preferred yellow moods to red ones. Yellow was the happiest color to her. She loved roller coasters, but she used to be scared of them. Every time she was in the car, she stuck her head out the window so she could be in the sun. Her favorite book was Treasure Island, and she'd read it so many times that the pages were creased by her fingertips. She always bent the pages. She was in love with the woods behind her house because she pretended they were haunted. She never cried in sad movies, but always jumped in the scary ones, and she never saw them alone. Her favorite song was Going to California by Led Zeppelin because it made her happy and sad at the same time. Her favorite shirt was a blue tank top with stripes and a coffee stain on the bottom left. She loved holding hands more than anything in the world, but was too scared to do it most of the time. She twitched her nose when she didn't want to sneeze and she preferred cinnamon gum to mint because the smell reminded her of autumn. I knew that she loved things wholeheartedly; either with all of her or not at all.

The only thing I didn't know about Parker was how she loved people, non-platonically. But even she didn't know how. She'd never done it.

Parker

At five fifteen, I rolled my pickup into the gravelly, sandy sidewalk that was Titlow Park. I knew that Josh would pick here of all places to come, but it was frickin cold. My hand was shaking as I slammed the door. Great. It was barely raining, but the sky was already dark grey, almost brown. I wasn't sure I liked it. I didn't feel safe.
But there's someone here who'll make you feel safe, my little voice whispered.
I didn't see the point in arguing with it. It was right. I thought about Josh's hugs, when he felt like giving them. Immediately, I felt myself smile.

I made my way across the street, across the train tracks, and down the sloped hill of sand until I was on the shoreline, and I felt the craziest feeling: I had this overwhelming desire to hug him. A real hug. Right now. I needed my arms and legs and neck and chest... everything. On, with, around, all. With him.
The wind picked up, but I wasn't cold. I scanned the area. No one else was here. Not one person.
He wasn't here.
All of the feelings I'd ever felt from being humiliated, embarrassed, ridiculed, or upset coursed through my head at that moment, and I wanted to melt into the sand and die. I'd been stood up. Of course I had. But from Josh? He was my friend. I thought...

"Parker?"
My head whipped around so fast at my name. He was crawling out from under the pier, shoeless and grinning almost goofily. My cheeks, which I'm sure were crimson red by this point, started to cool down and actually feel the weather.

"Sorry, I was under the pier. I didn't see you come down." He stated. Now, instead of feeling like an idiot, I was overwhelmed with a sense of relief and trust. Of course he hadn't stood me up. He was Josh.

"It's okay. Hi." I wrapped myself around him immediately, feeling my arms perfectly accented to under his armpits to the heighth of my ribcage that matched his to our waists that aligned to my cheek that rested against his sweater-and-jacket clad shoulder. And, despite it all, I could smell the trademark Josh- stale cigarettes and dusty cars and coffee, but now, the smell of lake brine and rain mixed in with it, creating a sort of- I don't know. A blue green smell. I wasn't exactly sure what to call it. All I knew was that I finally, actually felt safe somewhere that wasn't Charlie, and that was warm. Where Charlie was radiantly yellow, Josh was the best shade of blue I'd ever had and I wanted to just stand there and breathe it in until I couldn't forget it.

But he pulled away, and I let him.

We walked up to the top of the pier, sitting on the very very edge and letting our feet dangle between the rungs of the fence, our shoulders barely touching. I was semi-aware of how amazing that felt. What had changed? For a couple moments, no one said anything. He asked me how Antique Row was, and I told him about the roof and the coffee I got later on. (I was a sucker for Seattle coffee.) He asked if I bought anything. I told him just flowers.

"What kind?" He asked mildly. I knew what he was thinking. Either white lilies, for Charlie, or sunflowers, my favorite. He looked ready to be asked 'guess!'

But I was never one to play guessing games.

"Sunflowers. But only three."

"...Who only buys three sunflowers?"

"I do."

To which I got up and ran over to the little boulder by the road, where I'd hidden his sunflower. Keeping it behind my back, I walked back over to the pier, and sat criss-cross in front of him.

He smirked. "What'cha hiding, Park?"

I gently pulled out the smallest sunflower known to mankind, using my free hand to tuck a strand of escapee hair behind my ear. No taller than a textbook, it was without a doubt the sweetest, most innocent thing I'd ever seen. The vendor had said it was a mutation and gave me a good price. I handed it to him, biting the corner of my lip to stop from smiling.

"You're a good person, Josh. You've got a good spirit."
"Well, thanks. My spirit likes yours too." He laughs.
I smile. "What's my spirit like?"
At this, he frowns.
"I'm not sure of that just yet." He tilts his head just a little to the side, as if trying to study me better. "I'm still trying to figure you out. But as much as I know, it's beautiful. Happy. And sweet."
He pauses now, looking slightly embarrassed at having said too much.
"Yeah. Very sweet and happy. And nice. Like you. It reminds me of a sunflower."

"Park?"

A questioning, rushed voice, tinged with nervousness.

And in the millisecond from when he took the flower and looked up at me with that face I couldn't describe as anything other than just pure *Josh*, I knew what was going to happen, and I felt it, but I still didn't expect it.

Josh

I kissed her.
And it was the best decision I'd ever made in my life.
It certainly wasn't coordinated- I shot forward and just kissed her, hard and long, but not rough. Soft first kisses were just cheesy and overrated.
I held her face gently. I knew it was her first one. I wanted her to remember it- just Josh and Park. A good memory. She cherished and hated those, so I wanted to be a good one.

Parker

Nothing mattered at all but everything mattered all at once.
What are thoughts I couldn't remember
My mind was just one big WHATISGOINGON

How long would I remember this moment?
A couple weeks? A year?
I tried to formulate a single thought. A brain cell. Anything.
Okay he kissed me. He was kissing me. He *is* kissing me, present tense.
Josh was kissing me. My Josh. An actual kiss. A legit kiss.
It was so crazy and his lips were so soft and his face was perfect against
my own and I'd never known I could do this like this and I was so confused
but at the same time I wasn't, because it felt insanely *normal.* I wasn't even
sure what I was doing, honestly, but with him, it seemed like everything I
was doing was alright.
I would remember this forever.

Josh

She made this little noise when I touched her- like a gasp but not a gasp, a surprised little sound, and I loved her. And her hands shifted from holding the tiny flower to the sides of my face, to my neck, to my hair, and every inch and every second of it was wonderful. Her fingers were shaky but grew steady, and every second of everything was just pure and right. Parker was right. This was fireworks, this was bliss, and I was so grateful in that literal moment that this girl, this girl in front of me was Parker Russell and she was my Park.

Finally, we pulled away, and I saw her face- she looked scared. Her lip was trembling, red from where I'd kissed her, and her face was pale.

"Parker?" I asked.

She immediately grabbed my hand in hers, and I knew what was coming and I was relieved. She used to do this a lot. Whenever she was scared, she would grab my hands and pull herself into my lap and just go to sleep. I think she liked knowing someone was holding her and not going anywhere. She liked to feel safe. She liked to feel like she could trust someone. This was how Parker symbolized trust. Who could hold her, who could make her feel safe. She loved hugs. She loved being held. No one else held her but Charlie.

And now I was all she had left.

I dragged her onto me, and as I saw her hair fall over her face as she curled into a little ball on my thigh, I tucked it behind her ear again, pale blonde against rose petal skin.

"I'm okay, you know." She whispered aloud, her eyes closed. She was shaking like a leaf.

I didn't argue that. I didn't feel like something was wrong. I think she was just surprised.

It felt so, so good. She had to have felt that too. It was like- fucking fireworks, or an explosion or something.

It was right.

"I'm sorry. I don't know what's the matter with me. I didn't mean to mess everything up." She tried again.

"It's okay, Park. You didn't mess anything up. I just want you to be okay with *me*."

She nodded against my leg, then sighed quietly. Not a sad sigh. A content one.

"I am okay with you. I always have been. And-"

Silence. I waited for her to finish, but she didn't.

"Park?"

Parker

"-And now, the amazing Parker Russell!"
I am six years old. We're at my Grandpa Rudy's for Christmas Eve dinner,
like we do every year. I love my Grandpa's house- all lights and green and
red, laughter and good food. Little, adorable me is playing the grand piano,
as any small kid would. Slam all the keys, make as much sound as you
can. The adults around me are laughing, mingling, and holding glass flutes
of white wine. My father is in this crowd, but he is holding a black flask
instead of a glass. I would later come to learn that this was typical. His
drinking wasn't officially a diagnosed problem, but that didn't make it any
less awful for us.
"For our first act, we will have the star, Parker Russell, playing her original
on the piano!" I announce in a gruff, manly voice.
"Thank you, thank you, please, that's quite enough!" I respond in a lighter,
more feminine voice than my own, laughing gaily.
I rotate through the different characters unwillingly- the audience, the
announcer, and myself, all throughout my performance. I don't care if
people are watching me- I'm having too much fun on my own. Laughing to
myself, I proceed to finish my act.
"Well, that certainly was something, wasn't it?"
"Yes, Jerry, that was simply splendid! That girl has star quality!" I finish.
I rise from the piano, making my way through the throng of adults to find my
Grandpa Rudy. As I pass the hallway, I see my mother, talking rapid fire to
my father.

"She did what?" She asks concernedly.
"She was doing it again, in front of the whole fucking family. Doing her little-
the voices thing. Asking herself questions, then answering them. Different
fucking voices." My father replies in a quiet, barely controlled voice, wanting
instead to shout but knowing he can't.

My eyes rise up to meet theirs as they notice me finally, standing in the middle of the kitchen, witnessing their hidden conversation in the dim hallway. My shimmery gold dress I had waited three months to wear for Christmas Eve suddenly seemed less shimmery. I was being a star. Why were they mad?

My father's eyes were popping out of his head by now, and his face resembling a grape. My mother's mouth was in a thin line, her face drawn. "Get your things, Park, we're leaving. Go say goodbye to Grandpa Rudy." I promptly started to cry, all the way through the house, into the car, and all the way home, which didn't seem right because it was Christmas Eve. We hadn't even exchanged presents yet. I didn't get to say goodbye to Grandpa Rudy. In the car, I had finally lost it, screaming at my parents in my little voice, "Why can't you just be okay with me?"

I'd never yelled at them before. Which is probably why I got in the amount of trouble I did. I still remember exactly what it was. Two weeks without all my toys and books, and they didn't speak to me or acknowledge me. At all. Instead of getting the silent treatment, I got the invisible treatment. It was just easier for them to pretend they didn't have a troubled daughter, I guess.

When we got home on Christmas Eve, they said I'd better stop doing the different voices ("They're characters!" I wailed) because that was very bad, and Santa didn't bring presents to naughty little girls.

At the time, I didn't understand why it was such a big deal. It had always come naturally to me, to be different people inside my own head. It was scary sometimes, sure, when I was trying to concentrate or go to sleep and the whisperings wouldn't stop, but for the most part, it was fine. It was completely normal to me.

I was vaguely aware of my father's angry voice fading, fading, until it wasn't even his anymore, it was softer, and sounded more like.. someone else.

"Parker?"

I opened my eyes to see Josh staring down at me with a look on his face I didn't like. His eyes were dark, and his face was small.

"Yeah?" I tried timidly.

"You trailed off in the middle of a sentence."

I wanted to smack myself. Goddamnit, Parker. You can't just be normal for ten seconds? No, you have to be a fucking catatonic.

Wow. There I went again. Asking myself questions then answering them. I'm just a fucking basket case.

"Sorry." I said lamely, furious with myself. *Damnit,* Parker.

He slowly pushed away the strands that had escaped to my face.

"Parker? It's okay. You're okay. It's all okay. You hear me?"

He leaned his face closer, closer to my own, until I was breathing in his own breath rather than my own and his lips were that close to my own. *Hear me…. Ear me.. Ear me.. me…*

And then I summoned every single ounce of courage I didn't have and kissed him back.

And it wasn't perfect, but it was. I didn't care if it was perfect or not. I just knew that I wanted cigarettes and minty toothpaste breath on my own until the day I died.

Woah.

I really liked Josh.

The sky was so dark. It was so dark now. I was at Titlow beach, with Josh, at night. It was Tuesday. Charlie was gone. But I was here. Josh was here. And he understood, and he still liked me, despite it all.

Everything was okay.

"I hear you."

Lux

I couldn't believe it.

Almost three years. Almost three years. I hated the word almost. I hated all almosts. We *almost* lasted three years. We *almost* had a future together. We *almost* made it.

It sounded so pathetic I wanted to throw up then and there. This was an almost day, where an almost couple had an almost lasting relationship.

I paced my room up and down, trying to calm my breathing. I felt tears in my eyes, blurring my vision. I didn't stop them.

I made my way over to the end of my bed and sat down. My phone was still in my hand.

A part of me wanted to unlock it and read the message he had sent me over again, make sure it had really happened. A part of me thought I had dreamed it or something, thought that there was no way Mason would break up with me. Over *a phone call*. That same part of me thought that our relationship had meant more to both of us than that.

But that was a small part of me, and the more I thought about it, the more I realized that I should have seen this coming. Mason and I weren't perfect for each other, like I had so often imagined. He was kind of an asshole, self centered and rude. I hadn't treated him any better. I tossed my phone across my bed.

We almost made it. But, the more I looked at it from a one-sided angle, we probably wouldn't have lasted much longer than high school anyways. Too many differences, plus, once school was finished, the social castes would be abolished and we'd have to go our separate ways eventually.

Sure, we were a great match. I was Lux. He was Mason. We went together. We just did.

But the most important difference between Mason and I stood solid. Where he couldn't give a crap about his future, and status, and looks and all things

important and realistic, I did. Strongly. I cared about the future, it mattered.
Where Mason was a slacker, I, an achiever. We never would've lasted.
But he was still an asshole.
And I would miss him. Oh god, would I miss him.

But just there, as I stared at my my bed reflecting in the panes of my
window, daydreaming lazily, I spotted my phone, lying on my blankets
where I'd thrown it.
And it hit me. Who was the one person I'd always wanted, but never had?
Who was the one person I knew well enough to have something with, apart
from Mason?
I needed someone right this second. Parker was gone. Mason was gone.
Charlie- Charlie was gone. But there was someone else.
I felt myself smiling like a cheshire cat, despite everything. I sniffed away
the last of my tears, and carefully blinked the mascara out of my eyes.
Joshua Ethan.

Josh

"What is it, Lux?"

Her voice was rushed, a bit breathy, and a little winded.
"Can you come over? Now?"

I glanced at the tiny digital clock on my dashboard. Almost ten. Parker had left at seven for her therapist appointment.
"Yeah. What's up?"
A quick sigh of dismissal from her end. "I just- I really need you right now. Please?"

Lux had never, under any circumstances, 'needed me.' What the hell. She was probably fighting with Mason, needed some words of encouragement. "You can't call Parker? I mean, she's good with this kind of stuff...."

"Parker has a doctor's appointment, Josh! Please!"

It's not like I had other plans, although my brain screamed Parker's name. I could see her tomorrow, couldn't I? First thing in the morning. We could go into Tacoma for coffee. A perfect Friday date.
But this is something she would've done if she could've. I was here, Park wasn't: c'mon Josh, be a good person.
I found myself agreeing. It's what Parker would do. I should go, so Parker wouldn't have to feel bad about putting herself before her friend.

"Of course. I'll be there in twenty minutes, less if there's no traffic." Lux lived right on the harbor, which was only a short drive from Titlow.

"Thanks, Josh." She hung up.

I turned the key in the ignition, sort of half thinking, what the hell has Lux gotten herself into now? I sent Parker a quick text, asking what she was doing tomorrow morning, and took off for Gig Harbor.

Lux

I waited in the foyer, with just the right mix of nervousness, excitement, and promise bubbling all around the edges of my previous sadness and anger. I hadn't fixed my smeared makeup, runny mascara, anything.
Heartbroken. Wretched. Needy. Desperate. Not normally things I wanted to look, but I truly felt it. And I knew I needed them.
I knew Josh. I needed to make him feel like he was helping me, healing me.

Josh

There was guilt in my stomach as I walked up to the ostentatious door of Lux's house, somewhat inexplicably. Lux was my friend. I was helping her. I wasn't doing anything wrong.

I knocked three times. She opened the door seconds after, like she'd been waiting for me there. It was already obvious that something was wrong. Lux never waited for anyone at the door. She would wait, leave you at the door for just long enough that, for a second, you wondered if you had gotten the time wrong, if she'd left you in the dust. But then she'd open the door smoothly, smiling warmly, making you feel guilty for doubting her. She did it on purpose, I knew. She'd told me, when we first started becoming close friends, that she loved the idea of being fashionably late, and that it would probably have more of an effect if you were fashionably late to your own event.

"Leave them waiting, make them wonder. And when you *do* show up, it's like you're blessing them with your presence," She had told me, a distant gleam in her eye. That was when Lux was just Lux to everyone, not just me. Before her life was an act.

These days, she even seemed to pretend around me, and I only sometimes saw glimpses of the Lux that I had always known. The smart, clever, polished Lux.

But she had let her act crumble. I could tell, from the way she was shaking a little bit, and that her makeup had smeared down her face in little rivers. Her cheeks were shiny with tears, her breathing uneven.

Lux *hated* to be seen crying. The only time I could remember was when she'd fallen off the ladder at Titlow and landed on her back. But when she saw me, when we locked eye contact, the tears started coming again. She ran towards me and wrapped her arms around me and buried her face into my shirt and sobbed.

I was surprised. I had never seen Lux this open, this intimate. Not even with Mason.

The second I thought his name, I realized that's what was wrong with her.
Mason.
I smoothed her hair down and let her cry.

Lux

I hadn't meant to cry. But the second I saw Josh, looking at me with delicate pity, with sympathy, with something that Mason had never looked at me with, the tears came sprouting out.

Even if I had tried to stop them, I wouldn't have been able to. I realized that about the entire situation now, that it was completely out of my control.

"Hey," he said gently. "I'm here."

"I'm sorry," I said pulling away.

"No," he said, shaking his head but letting me slowly shrink out of our embrace. "Don't be."

I smiled gratefully, and took his hand and led him upstairs, past the dining room, past all the guest rooms, past my parents room, past my own.

When we had made it to the parlor (I'd dubbed it as the 'furniture room' as a little girl, being as we kept all my grandmother's old fancy furniture in here and no one could use it) I felt his hand pull away from mine slightly.

"Where are your parents? Where's Juliette?"

"They're gone this week in Chicago for Dad's business. Juliette's staying over at a friend's house." I smiled easily. I was okay. It was okay.

He didn't reply, but instead, I felt the tension slide out of his muscles and disappear.

I bit my lip hard to stop from grinning victoriously. This was going exactly as I had hoped.

The room was eerily calm. I opened the blinds on my window, then the window itself. The smell of the harbor washed over me then, and I was calm, and I knew what I wanted.

I stepped closer to Josh.

And I kissed him, and he had his hands on all the right places and I could feel his jawline against my cheek and everything was exactly what I needed it to be.

Josh

But... Parker.

I thought of her name a second too late, when the instinct to keep the human race alive took over and my morals, my beliefs, my feelings for her abandoned me.

Lux came closer still. I felt myself grow warm.

And she moved her way up my body, hands pulling me, tugging wherever they could reach, and I knew what was happening and I wanted it. I wanted Lux.

She pulled me against her. She didn't look upset anymore, just... intense. And yet she looked up at me, and her eyes were questioning me. *Is this what you want?*

My heartbeat quickened, I felt myself nod, and then she was pulling off my flannel.

Lux

A thought occurred to me right towards the end.
You can't keep kissing strangers forever and pretending it's him.
But Josh wasn't a stranger.
And I wasn't pretending to do anything.

Lux

I couldn't even help but be proud of myself. I am Lux Landry, queen of seduction and sultriness.

I got what I wanted after all. Josh. And, honestly, I was happier than I had ever been with Mason. Mason didn't hold me. Mason didn't do it that way….Moving on. Who needs all the fun little details?

I was happier than I had been since New York. The last time I'd been this exhausted, this relaxed... that was the day we went shopping in Manhattan. When we'd gotten home, Mason, Josh, Parker and I were sprawled out on Charlie's enormous bed, sleepily discussing dinner plans. I remember how happy everyone had been that day. How simply, purely radiant.

"So. Is dinner at the Smith okay with everyone tonight?" Charlie says from the doorway.

I have just gotten out of the shower.

"Is that the super fancy restaurant we were checking out on third?" I ask, wringing my hair out of the towel. The Smith had looked so good. Like somewhere I belonged.

Charlie smiles, his light brown eyes shining.

"Yep." His gaze returns to the rest of the group, to Josh perched on the wall and Mason in the chair and Parker on the corner of her bed. "If it's alright with you guys, I'll call and make the reservation right now."

I nod excitedly. I had bought the perfect dress today for the occasion, a sultry little black one, that dipped low past my collarbone.

Josh sighed. I wondered if he was awake. His body was so warm.

"Let's go to Rockefeller Center tomorrow," Charlie says all of a sudden. His eyes twinkle with the sheer thought of it. "Park would love the view."

We are all seated around our table, directly behind the bar. The lights are dim, the night is dark, and the food is amazing. Loud, alternative music blares out around us, and I feel so content. At home.
New York was definitely the place for me. Let the rest of them have their rainy and dull Washington. I would always remain here.
"Yes," I say to Charlie, "First thing." Parker lights up as well, and even Mason squeezes my hand in excitement. Josh smiles shyly.

Josh. I glanced over at him. He was definitely still asleep.
Josh.

Snippets of that day at Rockefeller center flashed through my mind, one by one by one.
I remembered it all, from the beginning, when the air was filled with excitement and friendship and sunshine, all the way to the shell-shocking ending, when my best friend was being carried into an ambulance, pronounced dead on arrival.
When Charlie killed himself, and everything just crumbled.

We are at Rockefeller center. I am in the bathroom, and Mason is too. Parker and Josh have gone to the snack bar and to pay for for the car parking. Charlie-

God, I hadn't thought about this in so long.
I mean, I had told the cops and paramedics what they wanted to hear, but I hadn't really *thought* about it.
I hadn't wanted to. I hadn't let myself.

Charlie has gone up to the top. Told us to meet him there.
I walk out of the bathroom, smelling like cheap lemon soap, and press the elevator button.
The up one.

The doors open, and Josh is standing there, looking like he always did. Unpretentious. Lost in thought.

Josh

Everything was so perfect.
After a little while, it seemed as if we were the only two left in the world.
The sky was quiet. Her room was quiet. It kind of reminded me of my own-
soft sounds, dark shadows, the moon in the window, a quiet place. She
might've fallen asleep, I wasn't sure. I was kind of sleepy myself. All I knew
was that Lux was in my arms, we were sitting on her enormous bed, and it
was dark outside.
And it felt really, really good.

But only a couple minutes after we did it- she was lying under me again- I
felt her tense up suddenly, as if she'd had a horrible revelation.
She opened her eyes, looking right at me- baby green against the
darkness.

"Josh?" Her voice went deeper now, almost.. apprehensive?
No. Confident.
Calm.

She took a breath that was too long for a normal question.

"Did you kill Charlie?"

She didn't ask it like a question. She asked it like it was her last words.

Lux

His eyes were dark and wide. Offended. Hurt. A little scared.
I immediately felt bad.

Josh

For a moment, I didn't say anything. Dead and total silence, for a heavy ten seconds.
But then it completely crashed over me in a single, concrete tidal wave of pure fury, and I was standing up and exploding.

"What the *hell,* Lux? So that's what you really wanted. That's all this was. You get me over here to comfort you and fuck you, but really, really, you just wanted to fucking *confront me* to see if I murdered our best friend? Wow. Wow."
She scuttled away from me, too slow, almost, pulling the sheets tighter around her shoulders, not looking afraid, not angry, not anything.
Then I saw the tiny glimmer of regret in her eyes.

"What the hell is your problem?" I yelled again. Was she out of her fucking mind?
I struggled to contain myself, feeling my fists ball and clench her cream sheets tightly. I dropped them, leaving a sweaty, tight indent behind.

"Lux," I tried more calmly this time. She was far away from me, on the foot of the bed, breathing too raggedly.
I tried to relax, despite it all.
"Lux. Charlie was one of my best friends in the world. My best friend. And honestly, murder? That's fucked up.
The police trust me. My best friends trust me. Why can't you?"

Lux

The pain starts up again and the worst part gets steadily worse.
I am in a bathtub… The tub is cold… my body hurts so bad. I'm so cold. I cry out, I scream for it to stop. But I did this to myself, didn't I? *I did this.*
I am so cold I want it to stop.
Slimy cloth, moldy, wet cloth is around my face, my eyes, it's dark, I'm choking, I can't talk now I can't see..
"I CAN'T SEE!" I want to scream, but I can't move my lips. I don't like the dark. I don't like this it *hurts* my back and my legs and my head, god, my head..
The cloth tightens, and I can feel the air escaping my lungs, I can feel my eyes start to dim I can feel the smooth marble on the pads of my fingertips as my legs stop thrashing and then it hits me…
I'm dying. This is what dying feels like.
Everything dims, everything fades.
Nothing flashes before my eyes, no moments of my life, no one, nothing, as my brain screams for air one last time, searing, searing pain, air, I just need one breath of-

The cloth tightens an inch tighter.
I stop moving.
And nothing is cold or hot anymore.

Josh

The chorus to Money by Pink Floyd blared me out of my sleep.

I could hear a younger Lux's voice ringing in my head.
"Pink Floyd? Really? You're such a stoner." She laughs, reading the back of the record sleeve.
Charlie raises an eyebrow. "That's a bit-"
"I'm right and you know it!" Lux says.
"It's been two years since I've heard this, and it still haunts me." Parker admits as Wish You Were Here begins to play. I don't think she's even paying attention.
"For the last time," I say to Lux, stretching out each word,
Parker jumps in then as we start to faux-yell together. "I DO NOT EVEN SMOKE!"
Lux laughs, throwing her head back. She's sitting on the windowsill. Charlie shakes his head, grinning, and Mason just snorts. My kid brother, Kyle, walks into my room and asks if we can keep it down, he's trying to play Black Ops. That just makes us laugh even harder.

It was the middle of the night, by the looks of it- maybe three. I fumbled awake, mechanically reaching over to grab my phone from the carpet. It slipped out of my fingers twice, and I swore loudly before managing to get a hold on it.
I unlocked my phone in a millisecond. Four missed calls- Parker. Oh, *shit.*
I dialed her number before my fingers even recognized what they were doing. She picked up within seconds.

"Josh, okay, holy shit, okay, okay, where are you right now?"

She was totally out of breath, crying too hard, and slightly panicked. No, entirely panicked.

I sat up, my heart starting to race too fast, too fast. It was crumbling.
I exhaled heavily, shakily.
"Uh- asleep. At home. What's wrong, Parker?"

I heard her inhale once, struggling to keep it all together, and then it all crashed and I heard her sob so loud and so childlike that I wanted to tear out of that house so fast and get to her right that second and just hold her, hold her close and tight.

"Parker!" I couldn't help myself, I yelled. "Parker tell me what's wrong right now."
Holy shit, I could barely breathe.

She finally composed a sentence that was understandable, amidst all her sputters and slight draws for breath.

"It- it's the police. Lux was j-just found, dead. She's d-dead, Josh, they think she k-killed herself."

She started sobbing again.
Lux was *dead?*

I heard heavy footsteps, and then my door flung open and my mom, armed with a puny kitchen knife, looked at me, just sitting on my bed, phone in hand, then breathed a loud sigh of relief.

I felt my head drop forwards. The-

Parker cut me off. "Josh, listen, y-you have to be at the s-station at ten am. They-they want us in f-for questioning about Lux's suicide. They think something's w-wrong."

Parker

The station was cold. I'd never been inside a police station before. And I'd always taken cops for the stereotypical, gruff kind of guys. Officer Johnstun was such a man. No-nonsense, quick to the point, loved his little grey mug of something that was probably coffee but smelled a hell of a lot duller.
As it were, we were interviewed by a detective, not Officer coffee mug. A seemingly young, mischievous-faced detective named Jay.
A detective?
He took us in for questioning one by one, ladies first.
Lucky me.

I had originally expected there to be some kind of bright, blinding light, or a hidden camera, or a lie detector, or something extravagant. I was 99% sure there must be hidden cameras, at least, but everything else was pretty mellow. The interrogation room itself was a box. A box complete with a table, three chairs, and a large wooden door.
They started off with the generic questions, name, age, where I grew up, that sort of thing. I answered them all. I'd stopped feeling numb after a while, and now that I could talk and function properly, talk I would.
I had the overwhelming feeling that there was something amiss here. The police planted that in my brain, but maybe I'd always known- there was something up. And that something resulted in Lux being dead.
I sat in a dull metal chair in front of an equally bland metal table. Detective Jay stood in front of me, but after the door was closed, he took a seat, smiling at me.
We started off slow.
"I'm Parker Russell. I'm eighteen years old. I've lived in Washington my whole life, but moved to Gig Harbor when I was three. I'm a senior at Gig

Harbor High School. Lux Landry was one of my best friends. I've known her since we were fourteen."

He nodded, writing everything down at lightning speed. He asked me things about Lux's home life and social life, and I answered them with unfailing certainty.
After about a half hour of intense discussion, he moved onto... Charlie.
I wasn't expecting that.

"So how did you know Charlie, personally? How did you meet? Were you two close?"

Despite my weak attempts to block it out, I found myself spilling over with warm memories, Charlie-yellow memories.
"Charlie is- was my best friend. I met him when I was eleven.
We were close since day one. I was bullied a lot, and Charlie was always, always there. He was kind of my safe place. We did everything together."

Detective Jay nodded and wrote some more notes. Then he paused.

"Were you ever involved with Charlie romantically?"

I blinked. Swallowed.
"Uh, no. He was one of my best friends."

But that was lying, and I knew it.

Snatches of our spring break in New York flashed through my head then, and Detective Jay's voice lowered to a steady hum before my mind selected the best and worst memory I'd ever experienced to settle on.

Charlie rolls over in his sleep, completely silent. Across the room, I can hear Lux mumbling and Mason snoring. Josh is flat on his back in his cot, his dark hair spilling over the pillow.

I turn over. I can't sleep. Maybe it's the foreign bed or the time difference, or the fact that I didn't eat enough at dinner. Whatever the reason, I have become a temporary insomniac.

As I turn over, I'm shocked to see that Charlie's eyes are wide open. Our faces are inches away from each other.

"Hey, Park." He smiles, god, that trademark golden Charlie smile I will never ever get sick of.

His face is masked by the darkness of the room, but I can see the faint outline; ski slope nose, long, dark lashes, and tan skin. Despite the weather pattern back home, Charlie had never fit in with the rest of us pale ones. He was born and raised in Washington, but I always liked to think that maybe, in a different life, he was from somewhere sunny and golden, like California, or Arizona, being a pro surfer or geologist or something. Somewhere like him.

His messy blonde hair is positively wrecked from tossing and turning.

"Hi." I say back. "I can't sleep, either."

He laughs a little, shifting his body easily to accommodate the space between us so he can look at my face. "How come?"

I tell him I don't know. He just laughs again, telling me if there's anything he can do to help, just let him know. He can make me tea or something.

I have the sheets pulled up to my chin, head tucked under. He reaches out suddenly, gently, pushing my hair off my face, and then leaves his hand on my cheek.

I feel myself glow with happiness. He's so gentle. He always is. He's my best friend in the world. Under his touch, I'm as safe as it's humanly possible.

He smiles again, closing his eyes as if savoring the moment. When he opens them again, he looks right at me and whispers,

"You're beautiful, Park. You know that?"

I duck my head even lower, sliding off the pillow, feeling so shy all of a sudden, because with Charlie you know he always means what he says. Wait a second. Why am I shy? This was Charlie. My Charlie.
I don't have to be afraid of him. If I was scared of Charlie, then nobody was trustworthy.
And I look up, and the moon illuminates his face and I can see him clearly, and I can imagine how this looks: two kids lying in a too-big bed in a hotel room, and the moonlight is shining down perfectly on just their faces and bodies, and he pulls her in close and-
Scene. It ends there.
At least, in the movie of my brain that's how it ends.
In reality though, Charlie sees this realization of no fear cross over my face, and he laughs, a Charlie laugh, but quieter since our friends are asleep. And he says he loves me, like he always says, and I believe him, like I always do.
And then he leans forward slowly, and I can feel my heart jump out of chest and my face pale, and he's holding me, and he is kissing me and then I'm kissing him back, because he's my Charlie, I'm his Park, and I love him.

As I snapped out of my memory, I realized this:
I had always loved Charlie. I had. Maybe subconsciously, maybe consciously, in some way, shape, or form, I had.
I always would.
I considered, just for a moment, telling Detective Jay this. But even in my head it sounded too sad. And saying it out loud was like admitting to the world, and to myself that he was never coming back.
But what hurt the most, I knew, was that I never got the chance to say it back. He'd said I love you that night. I'd never said it back. I'd realized only a month too late, and now, I would never have the chance to.

Detective Jay nodded. "Okay. Thank you, Parker." He looked over everything he'd written, then glanced back up at me again.

"Anything else you want to tell me while we're here? Now's the time to speak up."

This was it. This was the time to ask the questions I wanted- *needed* answers to. I thought about the last time she'd called me, asking to come over. I thought about the therapy appointment that I was originally going to ditch for Josh that night. I thought about my mom finding out I was planning to ditch and throwing a fit, resulting in my going anyways. I thought about everyone being conveniently out of her house that night.
My hands were clenched on either side of the chair, knuckles bright white.

"Lux- They found her in the tub, right?" My voice was rigid and tense.

"Her mother did. Correct."

"No one was around when it actually.. happened? Her parents were out of town..."

"As far as we know."

I found my throat getting tighter and tighter as my thoughts pounded at me faster and faster. Her family wasn't home. She was totally alone. She was never depressed, or in any way suicidal. It was just too *weird.*
It all spilled out then.
My voice grew louder and faster the more I realized what I was saying.
"And Charlie- no one was with him either. They told me that when they found him, his jacket was around his face, like a blindfold. And this too- when we were heading up to the top, he told us to meet him up there. Why would he say that if he'd been planning to kill himself? And with Lux, with the bath- the shower curtain was draped over her face."
I stopped talking fast. "If she was going to kill herself in the bathtub, why not just drown herself? Why suffocation? Who *does* that to themselves?"

The second I said it, something in my head clicked, and I realized I already knew the answer.

"Oh, holy *fuck."*
I teetered on the border of *do I pass out or do I throw up or do I just completely WHAT THE HELL.*

Detective Jay stared at me with a slightly mild look, completely ignoring my language, despite my shocking revelation.
"As far as we know, Parker, they were suicides. Weird, but still suicides."
But his tone of voice didn't match his words.
He paused, and this time, his voice had shifted into something much more sinister.

"But you're right. There was evidence of foul play in *both* deaths. We're investigating Miss Landry's right now."

My mouth was open, but nothing came out but a slight, hoarse squeak.

"And if they weren't- weren't suicides?"

I don't know why I said if. I knew now. Maybe I always had. My head was always holding stuff back, memories and recollections just barely balancing on the edge of consciousness. Maybe I'd always known Charlie hadn't killed himself.
The evidence was there. He'd never been depressed, or had reason to commit suicide. He'd always been our happy-go-lucky Charlie.
It was as if nothing was real anymore and reality was just one of my own hallucinations. *Charlie* hadn't killed himself. *Lux* didn't kill herself.
Someone else did it.

And then the fact, the actual idea that someone had physically *murdered* Charlie and Lux filled me with a white hot, blinding rage. I wanted to scream and hit the wall and just have a total meltdown. It was kind of scary, actually.

I struggled to calm myself the best I could.

The detective took a deep breath, looking pained, and leaned forwards slightly. "Then the Gig Harbor suicides were a cover up. A false lead. Murders, posed up as suicides, to cover the tracks. That would mean that we have a serial killer on our hands."

Josh

An hour after Parker's interview, it was my turn.

"Full name?"

"Joshua Alexander Ethan."

"Birth date?"

"August 12, 1996. I'm eighteen."

"Lived here all your life?"

"I was born in California and lived there until I was fourteen. San Diego. That's when my parents split up and my mom and I moved to Washington. We've been in Gig Harbor ever since. I'm a senior at Gig Harbor High School, which is where I met everyone."

The detective nodded, pausing to take a sip of his coffee. It wasn't even eight am yet. "Thank you. Now, tell me about your friendship with Lux Landry and Charlie Collins."

Charlie?

"I haven't been to the city in so long. I'm so excited that we're going. I love everything about it." Lux smiles, holding onto Mason's hand like her life depended on it.
I want to roll my eyes, but don't. Lux loves Mason, and yet the group remains intact. That was all that mattered. This group, these people. They're my life.

Charlie is driving now. We headed up to New York city for a little vacation. It's spring break, and New York City is beautiful. Parker had wanted to go during winter break, but her parents wouldn't let her, so the rest of us stayed behind too.

I'm sitting in the front, next to Charlie in the passenger seat. Lux, Mason, and Parker are squeezed in the back.
Parker is looking out the window. I can't see her face, but I have a pretty good guess that she's deep in thought.

I lean over and poke her knee. "Sorry we couldn't go during winter."

She flinches at my touch, but turns around anyways, a wistful look on her face.
"Oh. It's okay. I just love the snow."

"Yeah. Me too."

Lux overhears this and scoffs. "Washington has snow too, you know. God knows we get enough of it."
Parker says nothing to this, but smiles anyways. Who knows what she means.

Charlie lights up all of a sudden, and the car is filled with a warm glow. "Guys, there's our hotel! Wow."
And sure enough, it is. A huge, definitely more modern skyscraper looms over us, the brown and cream glass capturing every last of the sun's dying rays. Chambers Hotel: The Art of Life & Travel, the entrance portrays. Needless to say, it is beyond beautiful. Radiant might have been a better word. It all seems too perfect. With the sun setting, the lights of the city slowing getting brighter, and the safe closure of all the towering skyscrapers around me, I feel extremely at peace. This is definitely going to be a great week.

But I know someone else would be even more excited: Parker. She'd loved the city since forever.

I turn around, hoping to catch her smiling, or taking it all in.

She is staring out the window again. But this time, she has the window rolled down, head out, looking all around and up and down, and the look on her face is one of pure wonder. She's looking at this city like it's an angel descending from Heaven. She looks blissful, she looks passionate.

It was beautiful, watching the way her chalky blue eyes never stop moving, taking in all the skyscrapers and vast array of people and lights and cars. The black sky only adds to the hundreds of reds and blues and yellows and greens and purples that illuminate the city. Her light blonde curls are a mess in the wind, but she doesn't look like it's bothering her much. This was definitely where Parker belonged.

Charlie pulls up to the valet parking, and even he looks almost pained as he gently tells Parker it was time to get out.

At the door, an employee in a fancy suit greets us warmly, like the hotel got common teenagers like this all the time. We walked through the lobby, all of us knowing exactly how we looked in that one little moment: young. Fun. Alive.

I really liked that nothing was ever weird with this group. Literally anything. We'd wanted to all share one room, because, obviously, this wasn't going to be a cheap trip. So, naturally, Lux and Mason would be sharing a bed. That would be great once night time rolled around. Parker had automatically chosen Charlie.

Funny. I had thought for sure she'd have chosen me. I don't know why. I thought Charlie and I were equal to Parker.

Whatever.

So Charlie had agreed to all this, but also brought up the point "what hotel has three beds in one room?"

So it was fortunate that when Charlie had been browsing the hotel's website online, he selected the "Studio Double" room. The description said it had two king sized beds, a couch that doubled as another small bed, and

various desks, beds, and showers throughout. Luxury was what we were after. It was New York City, after all.
But when he unlocked the door to our room, I was taken back. It was completely and utterly ostentatious. The windows were floor to ceiling. The beds were colossal. There were comfy little armchairs scattered throughout the room, each one with it's own mini pillow and throw. It was the epitome of luxury and grace.

Parker strode over to the window and shyly opens the enormous grey curtains, soaking in the whole city view. I recall that when Charlie had been booking rooms, Parker specifically requested that their room have a nice view of the city. Charlie agreed, of course, and proceeded to go out of his way to find the room with the best view.

She looks so small, I thought. One hand clutching tight to the curtain, one crossed across her chest. Against the vivid backdrop, Parker's silhouette was just a star in the sea of galaxies and skyscrapers and lights. Except the funny thing was, she still looked like she belonged.

"Like the view, Park?" Charlie asks, smiling.

Parker's gaze breaks away from the window, and she laughs. Whether it was at herself or at Charlie, I couldn't tell.
"Oh my god, yes! It's perfect. Thanks, Charlie."
She darts over and gives him a warm hug, a Parker kind of hug. She always squeezes tight and holds on for a second too long. She doesn't usually show much emotion, but when she does, it's beautiful. Charlie just smiles, and I could tell he is pleased with her reaction. He's always making her happy.
Because when Parker was happy, everyone else was too. She'd always had that ability to brighten a room with nothing but herself.

"Now, where were you at 2:16 am yesterday on Sunday, April 16th?"

"I was in my room, asleep until Parker called me. Didn't my mom vouch for me?"

The detective took some quick notes, then looked at me with a strange glance. I didn't blink. I didn't falter. If he thought something was up with me, then he was fucked up too. It kind of pissed me off, honestly.

"Did Lux Landry have any reason to kill herself? Any previous history of depression, suicidal thoughts, or previous suicide attempts?"

I leaned back in my chair easily, the thoughts coursing through me fast, like summer lightning.
"No. She didn't. Lux had everything she ever wanted."

He now took his time glancing over me, slowly and intentionally.
"Son, you know she didn't *drown* herself in that bathtub, right? The shower curtains were tightened around her face. She suffocated to death."

I shrugged. This was too fucking intense and too-fucking-batshit-*crazy*.
"Yeah, that's messed up. But what's that supposed to mean? And hey, who even found her?"

Detective Jay ignored my question, leaning forward on his desk, his elbow nearly missing his coffee cup. He had a sick sort of grin plastered onto his shaven face.
"'So what?' You tell me."
He reached behind his desk and produced a clean manilla folder. He slapped it on the desk in front of me, the sickly grin replaced with a beautifully carved poker face.

"This is the police reports on the deaths of Charlie Collins and Lux Landry. Now, normally when someone commits suicide, the police don't investigate. There's no crime. But recently, our team in New York, and our local force here have been gathering evidence. There's foul play, kid. In both deaths, there was suspicious patterns.
In both deaths, the victims eyes were covered. In both deaths, they were seemingly alone. In both deaths, neither victim was suicidal.
"Suicides don't usually follow patterns. You know who follows patterns, son? Serial killers."

I remembered Lux asking me. "Did you kill Charlie?"
I remembered how hurt she look after she said it.
I remembered how hurt I felt after she said it.
I felt myself choke, and couldn't stop the coughing fit.
"I'm sorry, what?"

What? The? Fuck?

Detective Jay takes the death reports back. "What I'm saying, Mr. Ethan, is that it's becoming more and more clear to us that your friends didn't kill themselves. They were murdered."

Mason

I sat perfectly straight in my chair. This might actually be the craziest day in my life, and that was saying something.

"You're saying our friends were murdered?" I asked clearly, calmly. I couldn't wrap my head around this. I wasn't crying, I wasn't hysterical; I was collected.

Two police officers were seated around a long, rectangular table in a back room, with Parker, Josh, and all of our parents seated around the other side, officials and commoners separated by a chunk of wood.
Charlie's parents were stock still, and clutching each other's hands for dear life. Lux's parents, having rushed back from Chicago on hearing their daughter was found dead in her bathtub, were seated next to me. I couldn't tell if they either hated my guts or were just too lost in grief. I heard Juliette was being babysat and refused to leave her room.
My parents were on my other side, and my mom just kept crying and whispering that she loved me.
Parker and Josh were on the far side of the table, and if I looked close enough, I think they were holding hands. Yeah, they were. Josh's hand was in her lap, and she was holding it so tightly she was white. It was weird- it was like their bodies were in sync with each other, hardwired together, so to speak- when Parker moved, Josh moved. When Josh tilted his body a certain way, so did Parker's.
When did they become a thing?
Parker was frozen solid, the only thing moving were her eyes. Josh's too, but they were trained on her, then back at the police officer, then his mom.

The second police officer stared me down. I didn't flinch, but raised my head respectively. I was used to my football coach getting in these types of bossy, dominant moods. I could handle a cop.

"We've had our forensic team analyzing the deaths of Miss. Landry and Mr. Collins. The evidence is clear. Charlie Collins and Lux Landry were murdered. The only reason we didn't realize this immediately is because the deaths were classified as suicides right when they happened. There was no record of foul play."
Mr Collins was pushed off of a building, resulting in immediate death by head trauma. Miss Landry, on the other hand, was suffocated, a bit more.. violent."

If Lux were here, she would've just blurted out "Well who did it?"
But Lux wasn't here.
I swallowed heavily, looking the other way. I couldn't even tell if I was sad or not. Lux was dead.

"I'm sure you're all wanting to ask the inevitable- who did it?
But we aren't sure of that just yet. There was no DNA samples of a stranger, or someone with a motive. In fact, there *is* no motive that we're aware of. The only DNA was from you three."
Parker, Josh, and I all looked up.

Parker didn't even clear her throat.
"Of course our DNA was found on them. We're their best friends."

The cop nodded at her. "Right. But that means one of two things, and we already ruled out number two."

Mrs. Collins tilted her head to the side, clearing her throat.
"None of these kids killed my Charlie. They're good kids, officer. I know them all by heart."

"I know. So that means our murderer is a stranger to us."

After a few more heavy questions, the forensic team took the Collins' and the Landry's away, probably to discuss autopsies or something.
The remaining two cops eyeballed us three suspiciously.
After a moment, they trained their eyes on Parker and Josh, the world's most fucked-up couple to ever be.
Sorry. It's not my fault Parker has schizophrenia and Josh is just psycho on his own.
I'm so done with these people. Being associated with them. Charlie was one thing, he was a good guy. But everyone else... they're just so messed up. I don't even know why he picked them, of all people.

Cop number one stared me down, then asked the one question none of us had ever had the balls to ask ourselves.
"So tell me- why did he choose you three, plus Lux? What was so special about you that he picked you, specifically, as friends?"

As I swallowed dry air, Josh looked cornered, it was Parker who spoke up.

"He saved us."

The cop looked mildly surprised. "From what?"

She had to think about it for a second.
"Ourselves."

No one said anything.
I remembered the day he introduced Lux to us. Charlie, with his too-big clothes and winning smile. Parker, so small and timid, like she was about to break into a run at any second. Around Charlie, though, she was more relaxed.

Lux. Perfectly tailored since day one. Warm brown hair, warm everything. She was so *normal,* it was refreshing. But at the same time, she wasn't. She was polished like no other.

"Did Charlie have any people that disliked him? Maybe people on the side, people that you didn't know all that well?"

Parker was simmering. Her face, barely controlled, was absolutely furious. I knew she would literally explode if this cop said one more thing that insulted Charlie's memory.

He tried to explain, mistaking her expression for confusion. "Some homicide cases we get that are killed under suspicious charges dealt drugs on the side, or were involved with gang members that they had ticked off."

Mr and Mrs. Collin's both uttered a little sniff of disbelief.
Parker let go of Josh's hand.
Parker stood up.
Parker exploded.
"Charlie wasn't a coke dealer, damnit! He was a normal person who just happened to be more human than the rest of us. Nicer. Kinder. He didn't succumb to the craziness of the world like everyone else, which just made him better than the rest of us. He was just *nice.* Okay?"
And with that, she uttered a sigh of disgust and left the room in a whirl of anger.

Well. There goes the neighborhood.

Josh

"Parker!"

I threw a quick apology to the police officers and ran after her. Mason, still looking far away and ignorant, mouthed "she's your girlfriend?"

She was sitting on the curb outside the station, holding her face in her hands.

"Park. Hey. It's okay." I said, rubbing her back gently.
To my surprise, she stood up, whirling around on me with blazing, icy eyes and shaking limbs.
"No Josh, it's not okay. Stop saying that. Charlie is gone and *nothing* is okay! Two of
our best friends were *murdered*. Murdered. As in first degree actual murder. Do you get that? Does that at all affect you?"

I raised my face slightly, looking her in the eyes, keeping my voice calm.
"I'm not a sociopath, Parker. I grasp what you're saying quite clearly."

"Then why do you keep staying so controlled like it's not a big deal? Charlie was your best friend too! How can you just be calm and pretend it doesn't matter? Charlie mattered!"
She was yelling now. I never thought our first fight would come so soon.

"Because maybe it shouldn't be a big deal, Parker! Maybe we need to move on and live our lives while we can! We can't let this control us for our entire life!"

A very long, silent pause.

"Are you telling me to forget Charlie?"

Her voice took on a new tinge. Something… raw. Open.

I quickly backed it up.
"Wha- no, Park, that's not what I'm saying at all. Of course not. No. What I'm trying to say is that life sucks, okay? People die. People leave. But here's the thing. I won't be leaving you. You can count on that. I won't leave. You'll be okay. We have each other, right?"

She was quiet.
"He didn't want to leave us." She whispered, her eyes strong, but tired. "He didn't want to go. He didn't want to die."
She took a quick, hitching breath, tying herself together with an invisible string.
I rested my forehead against her own, and this time, I knew exactly what to say.

"When we have each other, we have everything, Park. That's what I'm trying to say here."
She just looked at me, defeated. She looked at me, and she dropped her arms, and she broke.

Parker

I just let him hold me while I didn't remember anything. I didn't care. This wasn't an episode, this was a missing.
I was missing a very large piece of me.
The piece that was my best friends. The piece that was the reason I was still here, literally, figuratively, and actually. Most girls had a boyfriend they attached their souls to.
I had Charlie, Josh, Lux, and Mason.
⅖ of our group were gone.
And I missed them.

And he just held me and kissed my hair over and over and over until I quieted down. I think he was whispering, too. Yeah, he was. He was saying I'm sorry.

"Josh?" I ventured after a couple minutes. Or eternity.
"Yeah?"

I hesitated. This had been on my mind for so long.

"Why- why do you think their eyes were covered?"

Josh never stopped stroking my back.
"I don't know, Park. Maybe so they couldn't see who killed them?"

I sighed.
"Yeah, I guess."
But what I was really thinking was much more insidious.

Because to me, covering a dead person's eyes was almost like someone wanted to leave them in the dark. Someone didn't want them to see the light. Someone felt hurt and betrayed and upset by them.

And while it made sense for Lux to have enemies- boys she'd rejected, girls she'd made fun of- no one would *kill* someone over something that dumb, right? This was the real world. People didn't kill people and get away with it. This was so real. This was so real. People I had known, I had loved, had been murdered under our noses.

Who would *do* that?

I supposed it made sense for Lux, maybe. But Charlie was the first to go. And Charlie had never hurt anyone.

Mason

"So. You and Parker?"

Josh had his eyes to the ground, not quite blushing or smiling, but not quiet poker face either.

We walked home from the police station after our interviews. It was way too tense to be around everyone, so I figured a walk to cool the air was a good idea.

He looked at the line of fir trees at the end of the sidewalk, then up at the grey, swirling sky.
"Yeah. Me and Parker." He said, almost to himself.

I chuckled. "When did *that* happen?" As far as I'd known, he'd liked her for ages, and had never once made a move. And it was always kind of obvious, if you were paying attention.

He shrugged, kicking at a piece of broken chalk left on the sidewalk. Two little brunette kids with messy hair ran outside, the girl holding a bucket of chalk.
"Maya, let me have the chalk!" The boy whined.
"It's mine, Lucas!" She calls back. She had chocolate around the rim of her mouth.
I smiled, watching them argue over who got the blue and who got the red.

"A while ago, I guess. I don't know."

I onced him over. He was acting so weird. Was he not excited to finally have a girlfriend? It had been long enough.

"Okay. Dude. I'm only going to ask you this once, because you're acting like a freak right now. Are you getting it?"

He whirled upon me, eyes bright. "What the hell is that supposed to mean?"

I smirked. "You know. Parker. You. Dating. Equals. Score. It's just the base system, bro."

Josh started to laugh. He laughed for a long time.
"Not yet. She's a little…. nervous, I think."

I fist bumped him heartily.
"Well, when you do, let me know. She's different, sure. But I can just tell, she's a wild one. I bet she's *insane* in b-"
"Okay. You can stop now."

Parker

For all the bad things I've done, (literally, actually nothing.) I still feel like one of the worst was that I showed Josh's mom more love than my own. Or, at least, more attention.

Lisa was seriously the kindest. And coolest. She didn't care that we just wanted to hang out in Josh's room. She had to go to work anyways, and remember to lock up if we were going out. Josh gave her the biggest hug and locked the door behind her, turning on the porch light.

Incidentally, we wouldn't be going out. We had a couple ideas in mind, all of which consisted of having the house to ourself, and just kinda relaxing. Maybe sleep. She also didn't care if I stayed the night- in Josh's room. Like, holy shit. I told my mom I was eighteen and would go to Josh's house if I wanted to. Despite her saying he 'wasn't good for me' and 'a bad influence' I could care less. She'd been saying stuff like that about him since I met him.

Tonight was going to be a good night. A fixing night. A perfect night. Just Josh and Park, in their element- dark rooms and closeness.

We'd been lying on his bedroom floor for maybe three, four hours. Not doing anything. Just talking quietly, asking things we'd never asked before. Not like we had to get to know one another, just little things. The little things we loved.

We had been steadily discussing what it would be like when we were grown up and far away, and it was making my head hurt. I just wanted here. I wanted now. I wanted what we had in this little moment to be forever.

I grabbed the hat off his head and fastened it on my own. Navy blue, baseball style, bearing the logo of some place in California. It just seemed right, in that moment.

"They don't get it. That's the problem." I sighed, glancing over at him. He was lying on the carpet, staring up at his ceiling that was full of black shadows and big blue stars.

He gestured for me to come over and put his arms behind his head, with me nestled in the crook of his arm. "Get what?"

I'm lying on my stomach, my cheek pressed against his chest. God, I felt so *safe.*

"It's just. That's the whole thing, with everyone, isn't it? We think we understand the world and how everything works. Real life. Suffering. Jobs, marriage, kids, travelling, why stuff happens, all of it. Karma isn't real, life is. We're all just kids playing at being adults, but even they don't know. We're smart. But we're completely oblivious to what reality really is. I think it's beyond us. We are clever but we're clueless."

Josh was quiet. Super quiet, like beyond deep thinking quiet. He was questioning, not thinking. He pulled the blanket off his bed and over our heads.

All at once, the pressure hit me- the room is so *dark.* The blankets were so *dark.* The shadows on the wall, the blue, green, and purple stars from the little machine, the bed, the clothes, everything. It's all so dark. So why did I feel so safe and warm?

No, those weren't the right words. Why did I feel so..

He finally broke the quietness of our minds.

"Is that how you really see everything, Parker? Dark?"

He sounded quiet, too.

"I guess. I always have. It makes sense. Darkness is real. It's predictable, most of the time. Like at school, I was in 6th or 7th grade. When these kids used to give me crap, I always used to fight back, but one day I just stopped. I don't know why. I just took it from then on out. And when I thought Charlie had really killed himself. That he left me, left me behind to deal with the tragedy he left in his wake. When my Dad gets in his moods and goes through a raging period. I'd like to think I didn't deserve any of that, and that sometimes, bad stuff just happens to good people. Suffering. It just happens anyways. That's the darkness. And it's real."

He was dead quiet.
"Like at that party in sophomore year?"

Josh

She shifted uncomfortably in my arms, and the look on her face was one of long-buried horror, a look that told me clearly that she'd thought about this so many times and was done. I had deep deep deep down hoped that that event would be so damaging to her mind that she'd just block it out and never remember it had actually happened.

Clearly, that hadn't happened. That party had been her second breaking point.

She faced me, looking... nothing. Flat. Dull.
I almost believed it.
Except nothing about Parker was dull.
"That was my fault, you know that. Don't dredge that up please."

"Park, it wasn't your fault, dammit. Don't say that. You didn't even have a chance-"

"Exactly, I didn't even have the chance! I was stupid, I should've just let it go already."

"You aren't *stupid* for not having the chance to get away. He fucking hurt you. He did that to you, knowing full well you'd have to live with that memory for the rest of your life. He's the reason you hate memories. He made you afraid, and that's not right."

She paused for a second, probably remembering that night, in all its awfulness.
"It doesn't matter, Josh. It's fine."

It took most of my willpower to not cry. Parker, lying here, no look at all on her face. Parker, not even caring.

I remembered that night almost better than she did. I remembered the house we were at. I remembered the brand of beer that people were carrying around.
I remembered the cup he'd handed her, and only her.
I remembered what she'd been wearing; a faded blue sundress.
The only thing I didn't remember was what the guy's face looked like.
I remembered how her face had looked.
Euphoric.

And that was Parker's weakness. She wanted to feel loved. That night, she had.
At least, she'd believed his act.
And that was why what had happened happened.
And no one, not Charlie, not Mason, not me, had been there to swoop in and save her.

Parker

He rolled over slightly, looking at me with the same dark eyes he had when Charlie died but now they were bigger, and said something that makes me sad but happy at the same time.
"Maybe the world is dark. But people aren't."

I didn't know how to respond to that.

"Sometimes I think it's my fault. You know how my dad is because of his drinking. I was no better than him. If I hadn't asked that guy to go get me a drink, nothing would've happened at all."
I looked over at Josh.
"Am I one of those dark people, Josh?"

Josh sat up, pulling me with him onto his bed. He sat directly in front of me, holding my hands tight.
"Don't ever say that again. You aren't dark, Parker. You fucking glow."
And then I remember him crushing me to him and just being held so tight and I said I love you, and he whispered back, he whispered *glow for me,* and he was holding me so close and our minds and our bodies were intertwined as one and I was safe, I was home, I was

Loved. I'm loved.

Josh

After how good stuff had been going the last couple times we hung out, I couldn't have been more surprised when it happened.
We were in the woods behind her house, 'camping.' Technically, all we had was a tent and some blankets, but still, we pretended like we were roughing it.
I hadn't actually slept in this tent since we were kids. Baby blue, and tiny, it was a bit more cramped now that we'd grown up a bit. Nevertheless.

It was almost dawn. The sky beyond the trees were streaked with pink and yellow, and even the tiniest hint of blue. Parker would want to see this.
As it were, she was asleep next to me, curled up in my grey hoodie and black leggings. She had to be freezing. Seriously.
I gently pulled her into my arms, hoping it would wake her gently. We could still sleep, sure, but I knew she wouldn't want to miss this.
She stirred slightly in my arms, until her eyes fluttered open.
"Morning, beautiful." I whispered.

She smiled, then burrowed her head into my side like a little kid. "It's freezing." She mumbled incoherently.

"I know. But look." I said, holding her tighter, gesturing towards the sunrise.

She loved it.

"Lux would've liked this." She said, almost wistfully.

I nodded. "Yeah. She would've liked mornings better, too. This tent is nothing. Her bed is a freaking ice cube at night."

Parker tensed up in my arms. Slowly, she sat up, rubbing sleep out of her eyes softly.
"What?"

I realized what I'd said. My tongue was stuck to the roof of my mouth. *Fuck.*

Parker stared at me, and I could feel her eyes growing lighter as they got colder.
"And how would you know that, Josh." She said, her voice barely warm.

Okay, fuck. Could I pass this off? She could've told me, maybe?

"Park, it was nothing. I was just-"
I trailed off, feeling my head get heavier and heavier.

Her eyes were blazing.
"No, Josh, no. Finish that sentence. What were you going to say?"

I took a deep breath. Maybe I could still salvage this day. Tell the truth, apologize relentlessly, do whatever she wanted. Crap.
"I was. Um. With Lux. The night Mason and her broke up."

Parker was silent for a long time, staring at my knees.
Then she looked up at me, her voice as melodic as ever, but hoarse now, as if she'd been yelling for hours, and my heart broke all over again.

"Did you sleep with her?"

"I- what?"

She had no expression at all now. "I asked you if you slept with her."

"Parker-"

"Damnit Josh, answer me!" She suddenly yelled, but her voice was still scratchy and it sounded off. I heard a snap in the bushes. I wondered if she'd scared off a bird or something.

Our knees were still touching. She didn't pull away.
"I- yes. I did."

Kissing Parker at Titlow.
Holding her in the car.
Breathing in her hair.
Listening to quiet music.
Counting the stars.
Every freckle is a star in itself.
Cinnamon and cocoa scented chest.
Feeling safe.
Feeling at home.

What the hell have I done?

And she was yelling "Of course you fucking did. But that's so typical of you, isn't it Josh, because that's all you really wanted. You couldn't get it from me, so you used her. Jesus Christ, you're all the same."

I yelled back. "It wasn't like that! She was upset and I didn't mean for it to happen but it did and-"

"Bullshit you didn't *mean it* to happen. You could have said no. A simple no and she would've backed off."

I was so pissed now.

"You didn't say no to that guy. How is this fair?"

I immediately regretted it. Fuck fuck *fuck.*
I didn't get a chance to take it back. Parker was absolutely livid. Her eyes were sparking and her face was bright red. I'd never seen it that red.

"I WAS UNCONSCIOUS, JOSH! I WAS FUCKING UNCONSCIOUS BECAUSE OF WHAT HE DID TO THE DRINK AND YOU KNOW THAT."
Her chest was heaving, she was almost reaching she was breathing so hard.

She continued,
"You knew that I wouldn't be able to do stuff like that because it would freak me out because all I've known is that sex comes with BEING FUCKING TERRIFIED, JOSH. ALL I'VE KNOWN IS THAT IT HAPPENED WHEN I DIDN'T WANT IT TO AND I WAS SCARED. You knew that. But you had to get it some way, so you got Lux and whatever we had was just shoved off to the side like it never mattered. Am I that replaceable?"

Parker stood up, yanking her boots on as hard as she could.
"Parker. Please. Just-"
Before I could even form the word 'wait,' she was gone.

Parker

Joshua *fucking* Ethan.

I stormed into the house, so glad my parents were gone.
I wasn't even sure what I felt. I felt angry. I felt upset. I felt confused.
I felt so fucking *awful.*
He'd lied to me. He'd never lied to me.
He fucking slept with her.
I wasn't sure why it hurt so much, but it did.
I felt used. And lied to. If he was with Lux that night, what else had he lied about?

Then my stomach dropped, and my anger almost vanished.
He'd lied to the police, too. Not just me.
Wasn't lying to the police a crime? A felony?
Maybe he was just scared, I thought. Scared of… what? Being suspected as a murderer? That was ridiculous. This was *Josh.* My-
I wasn't even sure what he was right now.
I leaned against the front door, warm air blasting onto my head as the heater kicked on, numbing my frozen, frozen body.
Josh.
Josh.

And then I thought this.
Maybe we're just born cold.

I thought about Rockefeller center. Where he'd been when Charlie went to the top.

"Hey, Park, I'm gonna go lock the car up. You good?"

"Yeah. I'm going to the snack bar. Want anything?"

"No thanks. See you in a bit."
He sort of smiles, waves, and then gets into the elevator.

I blinked.
At the time, it hadn't even occurred to me why he'd gotten into the elevator.
To go lock up the car. Duh.
But we were on the ground floor.

I felt hard, fast bile rising up into my throat. Disgusted with myself, I forced myself to swallow shakily, and consider what I was thinking here. I was so sick of myself and sick of my head.
And the more I thought about it, the more I realized I already knew.

A doctor's voice. *"She's experienced severe post traumatic stress..."*
Stress... ess... ess....esss
His voice. *"She's really in shock Officer, what should we do...."*

His voice. *"Parker wake up open your eyes come on get off the street..."*

Charlie. *"It's okay, Park. Just like this. Kiss your thumb. That's how you kiss someone. Just like that. It's okay, love.."*

Me.*"Where is Charlie?"*
Arlie... lie...lie...lie
Him. *"Maybe we should forget him!"*

And it all fell into place in that moment.
I loved Josh. I was in love with him.

But I knew what had happened.
I knew what happened to them.

I was violently sick to my stomach as I pictured it all. I didn't even try and make it to the sink, I threw up everything right there on the floor, hands and knees, so freaking *sick* of everything.
And then, I think I collapsed. I'm not entirely sure. I just remember setting the phone down on the table and standing there until everything was black, and my head hurt and there was whispering all around me, voices that weren't mine and yelling, anger, and yelling and crying and people and it was so loud I couldn't think anymore. I didn't want to.

I walked into the hallway.
I picked up the phone from the coffee table.
I dialed three numbers.
I waited.
A man answered.
I don't remember how his voice sounded.

"I'm so sorry to bother you this early," I remember saying.
"My name is Parker Russell. I have information on the murder of Charlie Collins."

four weeks later

Parker

I've been in the hospital for almost a month.
It was a lot worse than last time. When I was first diagnosed with schizophrenia, I was only six. When I was twelve, it got so bad I had to go to the hospital for a week. This time, I was kept on long term. It's almost been a month. A whole month of not knowing anything.
The first doctor told me that I was on the side of the road, by the cemetery where Charlie was buried when the police found me. I was laying on my side, in a ball, and shaking. I was totally catatonic and unresponsive, talking to myself. They weren't sure what was wrong with me or who I was, so they brought me to the emergency room in Gig Harbor. After a day, and talking with my parents, they sent me to a psychiatric hospital in Seattle.
I didn't eat anything or talk to anyone for four days. Apparently, I spent my hours looking out the window and rocking. They weren't even sure what had happened to me.
After a week, I came around, and they got most of the story out of me. Then they decided to keep me in solitary. They didn't want me to know what was going on. They wouldn't let me call anyone or see the newspapers. I don't even know what happened yet. I just stayed cooped up inside my room, writing, and talking to different doctors.
Incidentally, I had a room to myself.

One day, after about three weeks, one of my psychologists asked me to come with him to his office. He said he wanted to show me something.
He pulled out a plain white journal, and after a few moments I recognized it as the one I'd been given when I got here. I didn't remember ever writing in it.

He flipped through it for a minute, then paused at a certain page. He then handed it to me and told me to read it.

There was writing, surrounded by a crude drawing of a face, and where the brain belonged, there was ragged and zigzagged staircases, knobs, handles, locks and doors and stick people.

I read.

"Inside of the man was a mansion guarded by gates. Beyond the gates and inside of the mansion was a painted room. The painted room had a door with a lock. The man was sleeping and had misplaced the key sometime ago. His belly turned at the thought of his quandary. He took a pill then went to sleep."

After that, nothing.

I remember we both stood quiet for a while. I searched his face for recognition, but there was none.

After what seemed like hours, he looked at me and said,

"What's behind your painted room, Parker?"

I said I didn't know, but it was a lie, and he knew it.

He let me keep the journal. I flipped through it a couple times. Most of the writings were illegible and too incoherent (fucking schizophrenia) to understand, but a few caught my attention. There was one that had a drawing of a man carrying an enormous knapsack filled with clocks, machines, and unnamed objects. I liked to think that they were memories. Written around the man was,

"And he carried every last piece of it. He carried it until it scattered itself across the contiguous U.S. And with every piece that he lost, he found more and more of himself in his loss. The hole in his bag made his task that much easier."

And, in all capitalized letters at the end,

"SHE HAD WAITED FOR HIM ALL ALONG."

I thought about that for a long, long time that day.
My mind works in crazy ways.

Later that night at group therapy, the same doctor explained a concept
which was oddly familiar to my first cryptic writing. He asked all of us to
share what the meaning was behind our painted rooms.
I hadn't participated in any of the groups yet. I was the youngest person
here, and I didn't feel comfortable around everyone.
This time I raised my hand.
"Doctor," I said then, "There was once an illusion of meaning in all of this,
but the meaning is lost."

And then his face flashed behind my eyes.
And the sentence SHE HAD WAITED FOR HIM ALL ALONG zigzagged
through my head.
Would I be waiting?

And then I started crying.

Parker

I padded through the long hallway in my tan socks, making for the doorway.
Everything here was tan and grey, and I needed some color.

Outside, the world was blue and green and enclosed. And really, really
cold. This wasn't even Gig Harbor cold, this was just plain
Seattle-in-the-spring cold.

I tried not to pay attention to the fencing around the perimeter. I didn't even
know what it looked like beyond that fencing.

Instead, I went looking for my doctor. Technically, I wasn't supposed to be
on my own, but screw it.

I wanted answers.

It was raining, hard, like I was used to when I stepped under the sky. I was
only wearing jean shorts and a long-sleeved shirt, and it was freezing, but I
loved it. The cold on my bare legs felt reviving. I relished it, leaning my
head back, and I felt myself smile for real, laughing at myself. Parker in the
rain.

When my hair was good and stuck to my head, and my shorts soaked
through and my sleeves dripping and my face beaded with droplets, a pale
contrast to my freckles, I looked across the flooded courtyard, and Dr.
Maria saw me soaked to the bone and grinning like an idiot, she smiled
right back at me and waved, like a friend that's an ocean away.

Parker

Dr. Maria stood over me, pen and clipboard in hand.

"You can leave, Parker, when you're ready. Your hold is up. You don't need your parents approval."

"Today. I want to leave today."

"This is the second time you've been in a psychiatric hospital for a major schizophrenic episode. You're stable now, but do you think you're ready? Really?"

I pondered this for a moment. I really, really just wanted out of this hospital with its fenced in walls and back to the real world, where I could order my own food and sleep in an actual bed and drive myself and be alone for five minutes and shower unmonitored- but I forced myself to think rationally. Everything that had happened. Everything.

Two of my best friends were dead. I was in the hospital.

But it was so close to over. So close. We were *so close*. I got this far on my own.

"I'm ready."

Josh

"Ethan. You've got a visitor."
I heard faint footfalls coming through the hall. The bars were opened. I was escorted to a different room, one with a table and two chairs.
The guard stationed permanently outside my cell said I had fifteen minutes, no physical contact, and if he heard any shouting, I would be in solitary for five weeks instead of three.
Who the hell-
No..
No. I wouldn't get my hopes up. What would I even say?
I am so sorry.
I am so, so sorry.

Was I sorry?
Was I sorry?

No. I wasn't.
But I was sorry for her.

Words wouldn't cut it.
Nothing could fix what I'd done.

Parker

I looked through the glass window before going inside.

He was just sitting there. He wasn't focused on anything.

I couldn't make myself say his name.
But I also couldn't stop looking at him.

I couldn't make myself love him again. I just couldn't bring myself to do it. I really couldn't.
At one point, I wanted to, as sick as that was. What he did to me, to all of us.
I just missed us. I missed him.
I did.

Then I forced myself to remembered everything.
I pictured Charlie's smiling, easy going face.
I pictured Charlie, hugging me.
I pictured Lux, always getting you coffee and a hug out of the blue.
I pictured all three of us, waiting in the SeaTac airport, boarding the flight to New York with radiant moods that wouldn't fade.

And the urge to go back to him was crushed entirely, replaced by something I'm not sure I ever wanted to feel.
I didn't want to ever feel *us* again.
And feeling that was the hardest thing I'd ever done.

I wasn't even sure I really wanted to be here. A sick feeling formed in the pit of my stomach, and I felt nausea wash over me hard. What was I thinking?

But then I saw his hands, and they were shaking, and I found my voice.
A steady voice.
My voice.
I opened the door.

"...Josh?"

Josh

My hands shook under the table.

My name. She said my name.
I look up, and it's her.
She came back.

Acknowledgments

There are so many people that contributed to this book in so many different ways, some that they aren't even aware of, and before I start recalling them all, let me just say this- I'm so grateful for each and every one of you. All the people that helped me, the libraries I dug through to research Parker's illness, the places we drove in Washington, and all the artists and albums and people and places and views and flights and words that brought me here, brought me this.

Charlotte Josephine Kehder, good god, you were there every single step of the way, every milestone, nearly every single chapter. Thank you for being basically my co-author. Thank you for picking up at the randomest times and helping me work through a character's dilemma instead of doing homework or the GeoTech lab. Thank you for not giving up on Lux, despite all those attempts to turn her into someone she shouldn't have been. Thank you for talking through scenarios for Josh with me. Thank you for believing in Parker, and for believing in me. Thank you for neglecting French homework and conjugating verbs for, instead, working on plot rollercoasters and potential title names with me. (Murder in the Big Apple!) We both know this book *would not have happened* without your constant help. From Katherine Pierce to the Himalayan Mountain Range & Menswear, California to Oregon, I love you, Lo.

Savannah Moon Nagy, thank you for always, always, always believing in me and my writing abilities forever, and for being the bestest friend this world has ever seen. Thank you for introducing me to Washington and all the places used in this book. Thank you for 72215, for Santee Lakes, for always listening and never leaving, and the Blackbear playlist that I listened to whilst writing this whole book. Thank you for being my Sav for always. You're my best friend forever. I love you to the stars and back.

Amy Mason, I love you with every single inch of my heart. Thank you for everything. You mean the world to me, and I can honestly say I wouldn't be who I am right now without you. You are hands down the best role model ever.

Ivan Martinez, thank you for the amazing picture I used for the back cover. Kristin Kopsaftis, you are the best in the world at everything you do and write. Lil worm loves you.

Elle, Sophi, Jack Holmes, Amber Holmes, Sarah, Lillie, Phili, Rachel, Rylie, Chris, Jared, Nicole, Trent, Emily Talley, Rene, Daniela, Jen Nagy, Tete, Emily Holmes, Julia, Quez, Elizabeth, Neiva, Siena, and Willow, thank you guys for being the best friends and influences I've ever had. I love you all and you're so very important to me.

A HUGE thanks to Natalie Wall for showing me the wonders of the PNW (and her positivity and hilariousness) through her amazing photos. You're an inspiration.

And to Schuyler (Sky) Peck- thank you for believing in me, just being your wonderful lovely self, and being the bestest, kindest human. The world is lucky to have and know you. Love from your sweet sister, Ash.

Erin (and Cory,) you already know most of what I'm going to say, but here it is anyways- This book is for you because I love you, and you're the big sister I never had. You have always been my inspiration. Being in your life has been one of the best things in the world that I am eternally grateful for. You were there from Katherine & Kyle, all the way to now, even after all the bad stuff. All of it. You're the best role model I've ever had. You helped in ways you didn't know of, you gave me great advice when I didn't think I needed it and when I did, and you really were the best coach ever. Not just gymnastics. Almost like a life coach. You're brave. Smart. And, most importantly- an inspiration. I hope I can be half as wonderful as you are when I'm older. I love you, Erin.

And Cory, you too are a truly amazing role model and a person I really, really look up to and respect. You give great advice and are always rooting for me. You're kind, selfless, and loving- and you and Erin might just be my favorite two in the whole world.

Sarah. I love and appreciate you more than you'll ever know. I love you as a little sister, as as a best friend, and as my hot chocolate enthusiast forever. Thank you for taking care of me, for loving me, and always making me hot chocolate and eating ice cream and seeing scary movies. I'm the Margo to your Quentin.

Josh. By now, you're probably thinking that the character in this book is you.
He isn't.
He isn't you, but he is, you know?
You really did inspire me, and I'm grateful for that. I'm grateful for you. Part of the reason the character is named Josh is because he's smart. He knew what he wanted most of the time, and he was brave when he should've been and cautious when he shouldn't have. He was clever. Clueless? Maybe a little. But not much. One of my quotes I was going to put in this book but ended up not using was "Speak the truth, even if your voice shakes."
Maybe he should've known that, too.
Thank you for teaching me the right amounts of brave and smart. Thank you for showing me the places where your mind wanders and spirit dwells. My spirit likes yours, too.
Rachael.
This book is for you. Maybe you recognized yourself in this book, just a little bit- in Charlie.
For everything that's happened, just know this. I'll be your Ash forever. I hope I can be just like you. Funny. Kind. Positive. Bright. Selfless. Strong. Loyal. Special. Beautiful. Important.
Radiant.
Thank you for teaching me how to radiate all things positive and happy, just like you.
You glow.

The Gig Harbor Suicides

Ashdon Byszewski is sixteen years old and currently resides in California. Except she'd like to reside everywhere. She got the idea for The Gig Harbor Suicides on a city bus. She loves writing, coffee, gymnastics, climbing trees, and exploring airports. Ashdon hates referring to herself in the third person but sometimes, (like right now) the situation just calls for it. She plans to move to Seattle or South Carolina for college and, preferably, attend the University of Washington or Oregon State University to become a journalist. Her biggest dream is to travel the world. (and also maybe radically reshape it at the same time) She certainly is a sucker for road trips. And maps. She firmly believes in maps.

Lastly, she would like to give a shout out to Looking for Alaska and Mosquitoland, her two favorite books.

Made in the USA
Las Vegas, NV
18 March 2023

69257468R00081